Doc the Bunny and Other Short Tales:

Further Stories of
Living Out
By Mark Munger

Cloquet River Press

ISBN: 0972005072
Library of Congress Number: 2005907397

Published by Cloquet River Press
5353 Knudsen Road
Duluth, Minnesota 55803
Edited by Scribendi (www.scribendi.com)

Visit the publisher at: *www.cloquetriverpress.com*
Email the author at: cloquetriverpress@yahoo.com

Printed in the United States of America
Cover Design by René Munger

Once again, for my sons and for my wife:
No man could ask for more.

Acknowledgements

Many of these stories first appeared in issues of the *Hermantown Star* newspaper. Over a period of eight years, I was privileged to write a column entitled "Living Out" for the *Star* in which I chronicled the daily joys and travails of life lived along the banks of the Cloquet River in Northeastern Minnesota. The best of my columns have been collected in two volumes; this book and its predecessor, **River Stories: A Collection of Essays about Living Out** (Cloquet River Press, 2002, ISBN 0972005013).

    I wish to thank my fellow writers and board members of the Lake Superior Writers, as well as my friends in the Northwestern Ontario Writers' Workshop for all their encouragement and support.

    Mark Munger

    Duluth, Minnesota

    June 2005

Table of Contents

Doc the Bunny and Other Short Tales:

Further Stories of Living Out

Stories from the Lake Superior Basin
Duluth, Minnesota

The Baseball Game

I was never much of a ball player. This story should convince you of that.

Dazzling sunlight touched the trampled grass of a sandlot situated on a slight rise above the bronze water of the St. Louis River. I was at Grandma Munger's house in Riverside, a neighborhood located in a far western corner of Duluth; a neighborhood that was created to house workers employed in the old shipyard lining the Minnesota side of the River.

Elsie Munger, my paternal grandmother, was a large robust woman who loved to feed anyone who happened by her old two-story ramshackle house sitting on a dead end dirt road in Riverside. She was a wonderful cook and a terrible housekeeper. A dusty, covered piano sat untuned and unplayed in the living room of her house. Most of her other furniture was similarly unkempt. After Grandpa Harry died of a heart attack, Grandma took in "boarders": single men who worked low-paying blue-collar positions in the western part of town. I don't remember the individual men too well other than a guy named John. What John did for a living, what his story was before he came to live with Grandma, I haven't got a clue. I do remember he wore smartly pressed work pants, had oily hair, a ready smile and that he seemed to tolerate kids.

The smell of fresh bread dough greeted me when I woke up from my night's slumber.

"Hi Grandma," I said through a tired smile.

"Hello Mark," Grandma Munger replied, her hands and wrists white with flour. "I made caramel rolls for breakfast," she added, tilting her very old head in an effort to keep her eyeglasses from sliding off her nose and falling into the bread dough she was kneading.

I grabbed a gooey roll and slathered it with soft butter. The caramel and walnuts glistened in the morning sun despite the thick coating of grease obscuring the kitchen windows.

"What are your plans for the day?" Grandma asked, rolling and unrolling the dough, the undersides of her flabby upper arms wobbling from the effort.

"The kids up the street want me to play baseball," I said before gulping down a glass of cold whole milk.

Nothing but whole milk, heavy cream, and real butter at Grandma's. At home, it was artificial whipped topping, skim milk, and oleo margarine. On reflection, I'm sure that the difference between Grandma Munger's kitchen and my mother's kitchen caused my dad untold upset but it probably staved off the early onset of the heart problems that killed his father.

"Be careful," Grandma warned as I stood up from the table, pulled my ball cap over my eyes, and headed towards the door.

"I will."

I don't remember the names of the kids I hung around with in Riverside. Because Grandma was old, she didn't do much to entertain me other than stuffing me full of food. When I visited, I pretty much was left to my own devices. It was either use my imagination and play with whatever toys I brought with me from home, or seek out other kids. Grandma spent her time doing laundry, cooking, and watching soap operas on an old black and white Philco television set. She and I didn't play games or interact all that much but I really didn't mind. I was an only child then, used to having my way. Playing alone guaranteed I got my way.

It was August. I was to start school at Piedmont Elementary the next month. I was five years old. I didn't own a baseball glove. I didn't know how to throw a baseball or swing a bat. But I was a body, an extra boy that the neighborhood kids could stick in the field to even up the numbers.

"Hey," one of the older boys called out as I kicked up dust walking along the gravel road adjoining the sandlot. "With Munger, we've got five a side. You're on the team that's batting," the kid said as he pointed at me.

The team in the field had a pitcher, a first baseman, a short stop, and two outfielders. All of the boys had gloves. All of them wore battered baseball caps over neat crew cuts. It was late morning. The day was already hot. Grasshoppers sang from the tall grass that began where the informal ball field ended.

I'm not sure what I was thinking as I walked between the batter and the catcher. A kid tossed a hardball towards a distressed piece of cardboard that served as home plate. All I remember is the sound of the wooden bat slamming into my head. Then I was out cold. How long I remained on my back with nine other boys clustered around me, calling my name, trying to get me to wake up, I don't know.

"You OK?" one of the older kids asked as my eyes blinked and I tried to focus.

"You're bleeding like crazy," a blond-headed kid added, his face close to mine as he kneeled to study my injury. "You better go tell your Grandma."

My head was thick with pain as I shook it from side to side.

"No. I'm not having her call my dad at the office. He'll be really mad if he finds out," I replied.

"You don't look so good," one of the older boys remarked.

I stopped crying. The tears dried on my cheeks.

"I can play," I added defiantly. I sat up. The sudden movement caused my head to spin. I thought I was going to puke.

"I dunno," the big kid who first saw me coming up the hill interjected. "You should go home."

An adult voice called from one of the little bungalows situated in a neat row across from the vacant lot.

"That's my dad," a blue-eyed boy of ten, the oldest boy there, said. "He's taking me and my little brother to the Dairy Queen. You wanna come?" he asked, directing his question to the entire group.

"It's too hot to play anyway," someone responded. "I'll go get my money."

Other kids stood up and sprinted towards their houses. The boy who had extended the invitation looked at my face and whistled.

"Wow, that's one nasty cut," he observed. "You sure you're OK?"

I stood up and I wiped dried blood from my face with the dirty edge of my T-shirt.

"Sure. I'll go ask Grandma for money. Don't leave without me," I implored.

The boy shook his head and raced off towards his house.

In Grandma's living room I stood quietly as Grandma Munger watched *The Edge of Nigh*. My T-shirt was turned inside out to conceal the blood and my ball cap was shoved down on my head so that the brim concealed the cut on my face.

"Danny's dad is taking us to Dairy Queen," I said when a commercial came on.

"That's nice," Grandma responded, her eyes riveted to the television. "There's change in my coin purse. Take fifty cents."

Grandma never looked in my direction. She didn't see that my shirt was inside out or that there was a large gash on my face spanning the socket of my left eye. I walked into the dining room, found her purse, and took the change she'd offered.

"Don't be gone too long now," she admonished as I walked through the kitchen.

"I won't," I answered, a headache pulsing across my forehead as I strode towards the door.

"What'll you have, Munger?" Danny's dad asked as we pulled into the parking lot of the Grand Avenue Dairy Queen.

Behind the tiny structure, the bell tower of Denfeld High School rose to touch the late summer sky. I knew Denfeld was where my mom and dad had gone to high school. I guessed, correctly as it turned out, that's where I'd go as well.

"Chocolate malt," I answered weakly.

The headache hadn't lessened. The pain was intense. I was having trouble sitting upright in the cargo area of the old Ford station wagon that brought us to Dairy Queen. Eleven boys were crammed into the car. Three of us sat in the back. There were no seats in the cargo area. We sat Indian style on the carpeted floor. None of the seats in the wagon had seat belts anyway. The auto industry was still five or six years away from supplying seat belts in passenger cars as a matter of course.

"What's wrong with you?" Danny's dad asked when he faced me to take my order.

"Nothin'", I lied.

"You're as white as a ghost," he observed.

"He got hit with a bat," Danny offered. "Right between the eyes," the kid added.

"What? Let me see," the man commanded as he swiveled completely around in the driver's seat. "Take off that hat," he added in a serious voice.

I lifted my ball cap by its brim allowing my face to emerge from shadow.

"Are you nuts?" Danny's father whispered. "You need to see a doctor. That eye is so puffed out, who knows how bad you're hurt. I gotta get you back to your grandma's."

"Can we still get our ice cream?" Dan pouted.

The man pulled hard on his chin with his right hand as he thought. Bright afternoon light cast a halo across the stubble of his shorn head.

"I guess that wouldn't hurt. We're already here. But we're heading back as soon as you all get your ice cream."

"Sorry to have to tell you this," Danny's father told my grandmother as he stood behind me on the bottom stair of the rickety old staircase leading to the front door of Grandma Munger's house.

"Front door" is really a misnomer. The stairs we stood on led to the home's kitchen. The house actually faced St. Louis River Bay. A covered porch cluttered with old furniture, dead houseplants in cracked pots, and assorted discarded items stretched across the front of the house. Because the main road to the place went by the rear of the structure, where an old garage leaned precariously to the west, the back porch was the only entrance visitors used.

"Mark got hit in the eye with a ball bat," the man concluded, removing my cap to reveal the full impact of my injury.

"Oh my word," Grandma gasped, nearly falling off the porch in shock.

My dad was called. He left his law office to take me to the doctor. By the time he arrived, I was trembling in fear.

"What's wrong?" he asked, urging me into the front passenger seat of his 1960 Dodge station wagon. "Does it hurt?"

I murmured something in the negative and hid my face in my hands as the Dart pulled across gravel, spinning its tires and kicking up rocks as we raced away from Grandma's house. I anticipated a long lecture from my father about the dangers of walking into moving baseball bats as we drove towards the old Duluth Clinic in downtown. Instead, the car turned left, away from downtown Duluth, as we exited Riverside.

"Where we goin'?" I asked.

"Dr. Munger's house," my dad responded.

Jim Munger was a member of our church but no relation. He worked for US Steel at the Gary-New Duluth plant as a staff physician. We turned into Morgan Park, a factory town built by US Steel. As we passed row after row of identical homes constructed of concrete blocks, I began to cry.

"It'll be fine," Dad whispered.

The reality was that things weren't fine when we walked into Dr. Munger's house. He greeted us with a black medical bag. My dad removed my baseball cap so the doctor could inspect my injury.

"Nothing broken," Dr. Munger reported as he touched the tender edges of the bruise that had formed in my left eye socket. "He needs a couple of stitches to hold the edges of the skin in place. I'll give him a shot of Novocain before I sew him up."

The syringe Doc Munger pulled out of that bag looked to be two feet long. When I saw the needle and realized that he intended to stick me with the thing, I bolted. It took the good doctor and my father the better part of a half-hour

13

chasing me around Doc Munger's house, with me diving beneath dining room and living room furniture before they trapped me behind a couch where Dr. Munger administered the dreaded shot.

When I started Kindergarten a couple of weeks later the stitches were still visible. I wore a black eye patch held in place by an elastic string to protect the wound from further injury. When kids at Piedmont Elementary asked what happened, I didn't tell them I'd walked into the business end of a baseball bat. I simply told them that I was a pirate.

Field of Unfulfilled Dreams

In the Piedmont neighborhood of Duluth, Minnesota where I grew up, there were a lot of kids. My buddy Eddie and I calculated once that in the three blocks we considered "the neighborhood", Chambersburg Avenue, Hutchinson Road, Morris Thomas Road, and Robert Court, there were nearly five hundred children from infancy to high school age living in that small piece of the world. This meant plenty of boys available for tackle football games against the Huard Gang (a motley crew living a few blocks away), or for ball hockey on a level stretch of Hutchinson Road, and, most importantly, for baseball.

When I was in kindergarten and first grade, the older boys in my neighborhood played baseball on a grassy field beyond our backyard fence. Sometime during the Kennedy years, the Catholic Diocese of Duluth decided to build St. Lawrence School and Church. Though the church never got built, the school was, its presence forever destroying the impromptu ball field. Eventually, after all their kids grew up and the Catholics living in Piedmont Heights aged, the school closed and the school's gymnasium, which had been used as a temporary sanctuary for the better part of twenty years, was remodeled into a permanent worship space.

One contractor constructed nearly every home in Piedmont. This developer apparently realized that the pent up desire of WW II and Korean War veterans to own their own homes was an urge that he could satisfy. The builder acquired land throughout Piedmont Heights and set about building homes for young families. Even though he constructed hundreds of houses on the knoll overlooking Lake Superior, acres of his land, land that had been logged off at the turn of the 19th century and converted into dairy farms by immigrants, remained essentially untouched.   Understand: There were no signs erected by the developer precluding us from using his land. And so, the Field of Unfulfilled Dreams was born.

We should have seen it coming. Despite the lack of "No Trespassing" or other prohibitive signage posted along the aspen and birch woodlands bordering Hutchinson Road, we knew that the developer wasn't especially fond of kids. Even so, all the boys in the neighborhood considered that the developer's land was open to our use.

Though Eddie and I were appreciably younger than the guys we hung out with, these older boys tolerated us. We served as batboys for their baseball contests and fans for the surf music jam sessions that took place on steamy summer nights in the older boys' garages. Given our past experiences with the developer, we, and the older boys in particular, should have anticipated the man's displeasure when we decided to "improve" his property by building a baseball field on it.

We'd stood by helplessly as our "shacks", crudely constructed tree houses built with purloined tarpaper and "borrowed" construction lumber, were ripped from trees by the man's backhoe. This destruction came even though he'd never warned us about building on his property. He'd never talked to our parents. He simply removed the offending structures and went about the business of building houses and making money, as if all of us, all the male children living in his subdivisions, didn't exist.

When Mike Urie, the Moe brothers, and the Milich boys, along with a host of others, decided to build a ball field in a meadow surrounded by thick aspens and birch on land owned by Piedmont's version of Mr. Potter (think *It's A Wonderful Life*), the longevity of the completed field should have been obvious.

Under the harsh light of high summer, Eddie and I joined the older boys chopping down trees, clearing brush, and doing what we were commanded to do. The project began in late June. Insects buzzed in the sultry air. I perspired as I worked alongside Eddie in the heat.

All of the supports for the field's two dugouts, a log backstop, and a homerun fence were cut from felled aspen by hand. In those days, chain saws were virtually unknown and no father in his right mind would have let any of us use one had one been available.

After weeks of labor, the ball field was ready for play. Two crude pennants made from old pillow cases, one labeled "home" and one labeled "visitors", flapped in the summer breeze. Nomenclature really didn't matter since everyone playing the game came from the neighborhood. The sides were picked one boy (girls were not allowed to participate) at a time by designated team captains. The captains alternated their picks to insure the teams were of roughly equal talent. I believe that Dave Milich, the eldest Milich brother, served as the umpire. I know that Eddie and I were assigned the task of making sure both teams had plenty of cold drinking water. We were also in charge of shagging baseballs in the woods.

I don't remember the score of that first game at the new field. I do recall the thrill of being part of something created completely by kids. I remember searching for lost baseballs in the alder swamp behind the backstop. I also recall that the boys playing in that game played to win. They dove in their blue jeans for ground balls hit across perilously rocky ground. They ran full speed for pop flies and line drives, disregarding the stumps precariously dotting the outfield. They wore baseball caps displaying the insignias of the Twins, the Yankees, and the Duluth-Superior Dukes, our local minor league team, and were serious about the game of baseball.

When we arrived at the field the next afternoon for a second contest, everything was gone. The developer had, despite our best attempts to hide our secret in the young forest covering his land, discovered the baseball field. The contractor's bulldozer made short work of our efforts. The fences were pushed into insignificant piles of broken timber. The dugouts were reduced to rubbish. The scoreboard, a piece of plywood that someone had rescued from the developer's lumber pile and attached eyehooks to hang cardboard numbers from, was broken in two and rested atop the debris. The carefully mowed infield, its grass cut short by a push mower borrowed from someone's father, had been bladed by a dozer.

The resulting ridges rendered the infield useless for future contests.

The boys of the neighborhood stood in raw sunlight staring in disbelief at the carnage. A lesson regarding powerful men and their tendencies was revealed to us that morning, a lesson repeated all too often in history.

Studying Up

The year was 1978. It was getting on towards summer. I'd proposed to my girlfriend, a woman with big brown eyes and a quick wit, on New Year's Eve of 1976. I was surprised that she saw anything in me worth accepting but accept me she did. I graduated from the University of Minnesota-Duluth and moved to the Twin Cities to start law school. René stayed in Duluth to work on her art degree. It was a long year.

Law school courses are often taught by bull-headed narcissistic jerks who, though they've never tried a case in court, act like they have all the answers. Intricacies of legal theory are conveyed to stupefied pupils by way of the Socratic Method. Boiled down to the barest of principles, the Socratic Method is calculated to demean and ridicule the students in attendance. Some folks take naturally to abuse and excel under such conditions. I'm not configured that way.

During my first semester at William Mitchell College of Law, I followed law school protocol and joined a study group as soon as classes began. Study groups, small clusters of students in the same section of a first year class, were meant to ease the pain of the Socratic Method, a sort of group therapy. At least, that's how the concept was billed. After a week of meeting with other shell-shocked "One L's" (first year students), I figured out that study groups were really designed to further the dissection and destruction of the weak at the hands of the confidant. A first year student brimming with self-assurance would take command of the group and dominate his or her terrified classmates.

"I think the holding in the *Myers* case stands for the proposition that negligence is a function of breach and duty," I had urged.

"Interesting," our group leader said. "Anyone else share Mr. Munger's tortured view of the case holding?"

A lump formed in my throat. I'd graduated from college with honors. I was working full time to pay my way through law school. I was apprehensive and on the verge of

19

bolting, leaving St. Paul for the safety of my hometown and folks I knew, folks that thought I was above average. I stared at the members of the group. No one was ready to go to bat for me. I knew that I had to get out, to go it alone.

By the time René came to visit William Mitchell in the spring of 1978, I'd managed to struggle through a full semester of law school with mediocre grades. I'd disassociated myself from all campus organizations. I was pretty much stumbling through classes on my own. When my fiancée came to town, I'm not sure why I decided to bring her to class with me.

"You want to sit in on one of my classes?" I asked her over "all you can eat lunch" at Shakee's Pizza.

"Sure."

"I've got Contracts tonight."

"Contracts," she repeated before sipping on a Coke, "sounds exciting," she completed in deadpan.

Homework for law students consists of reading cases, outlining the written decisions, and being prepared to discuss the holdings and theories of law behind the judicial opinions. It's grueling, time-consuming work. The outlining is done with hi-lighters, which mark up the relevant text. These notations make used course books either more or less valuable depending upon whether the last person to own the book was a good student or a moron. Despite the fact that I was working full time for the State of Minnesota as a consumer complaint investigator during the day, and going to school four nights a week, I generally finished most of the required course work before class; the operative word being "generally."

"Professor Goldberg, this is my fiancée, René. She'll be sitting in on your class tonight if it's OK."

Mel Goldberg was a Jewish man with insubstantial red hair, a significant red beard, and pronounced girth. He was an excellent teacher and fair to a fault. He used the Socratic Method but applied it with uniformity and a just hand.

"That's fine. Have her sit next to you. Just move Mr. Michelson over a seat."

Bill Michelson sat next to me in every class I had during first year. We became good friends. Bill and his wife Caroline lived in an apartment not far from mine in Bloomington, in the shadow of old Metropolitan Stadium. Many nights they invited me over for steaks on the grill, instinctively knowing that my roommate, an avowed Finlander and stingy to the bone, had eaten the last of our canned tuna.

"Hi René," Bill said as my wife-to-be and I slid into chairs in the third row of seating in the classroom.

There were four levels of student seating rising from the front of the lecture hall to the windows at the rear of the classroom. Soft light infiltrated the space as Professor Goldberg took his place at the lectern in front of over one hundred aspiring lawyers.

"Hi, Bill," René responded quietly.

We opened our contracts textbooks to the appropriate page. Despite my fiancée's presence, I was calm, ready to display my legal knowledge to impress the woman I loved, in front of an audience of smug overly confidant wanna-be lawyers. The class flew by. I waited to be called upon. Mel plowed through case after case, never once looking in my direction or mentioning my name.

In the midst of closing my text in anticipation of dismissal, a horrible reality descended. There were five minutes left in the class. I double-checked the assignment against my outline. I'd missed the last case assigned.

He'll never call on me, I postulated. *He probably won't even get to the last decision.*

Then it happened. With over a hundred fellow students looking on, with René sitting right next to me, smack dab in the middle of the crowd, I heard these words:

"Regarding the case of *Cowles Industries v. Newstrom,* Mr. Munger, would you lead the class through the facts, opinion, and holding?"

Panic gripped me. My eyelids clenched. Sweat began to flow down the flanks of my chest. I looked at René. There was no recognition in her eyes. She had no clue what was about to happen.

21

In retrospect, it seems like I stared at Professor Goldberg for eternity but I'm now certain that the delay in my response was only momentary. I imagine it seems longer because, when your head is on the chopping block, time stands still.

"Ah," I mumbled, "I'm not prepared on that one, Professor Goldberg."

A look of disappointment clouded the instructor's face. His small eyes burned right through me. I tried to escape his scrutiny. There was no place to hide.

Rodents

It was early autumn, 1984. My wife René and I made a few discoveries after moving to Fredenberg Township from the city. These revelations included, in no particular order: that the tiny dairy barn located on the property was full to the brim with sheep dung; that the Drews (the former owners of the place) planted more strawberries on the place than a small village could harvest; and that the Cloquet River, at least as it flows by our land, stays cold all summer long. We also learned something about rodents.

As a kid growing up in the Piedmont Heights neighborhood of Duluth, I encountered my share of moles and field mice. And I saw, from time to time as I walked through the city's West End, the odd Norwegian rat scurrying across the pavement. In fact, when the State of Minnesota demolished numerous old homes along Piedmont Avenue during the early 1970's to make way for I-35, thousands of homeless rats migrated uphill in search of shelter. Some of them made it to my childhood home located on the banks of Miller Creek.

You might be put off by the thought of migrating rats. You should be. But even vermin can have their humorous aspects.

Pelly, my brother Dave's Golden Retriever, was just a pup when the last of the rats crested the hill and found their way into the creek bottom behind our house. I began seeing the departing hindquarters of the rodents each morning when I'd walk outside to feed Pelly. It seems that rats love dog kibble. Through the course of that winter, more and more rats arrived to dine on Pelly's food.

Nature has a way of dealing with over population. A snowy owl took up residence in a balsam tree outside our kitchen window. The bird began snacking on rats bold enough to show their fur. The winged predator began to decimate the rodent minions. Though the owl's predation was effective, it wasn't easy eating my breakfast as the owl ripped up a dead rat immediately outside the kitchen window. But the bird got the job done. It was the perfect situation until the bird attempted to snack on my sister Annie's toy poodle. The bird's talons left permanent scars on the dog's skull. The poodle refused to go outside for weeks.

One winter morning, as I trudged through the shifting snow between my parent's garage and the dog kennel, I witnessed an amazing scene. Pelly reclined in the shadows of his doghouse. As I approached, I saw a fat Norwegian rat perched in the middle of Pelly's food dish chewing kibble. Before I took another step, the retriever dove from cover, snapped his jaws, and caught the rat. To his credit, the dog didn't attempt to eat the thing. He simply left the dead animal in the food dish for my disposal. After that, I never saw another rat around my parent's place. They must have gotten the message and moved on.

Years later when my wife René, Matthew, our first-born son, and I moved to the country, it didn't take too many evenings of watching deer mice, field mice, and voles parading across the abused shag carpeting of our living room to figure out that rodents were the real owners of the farmhouse.

Squeak.

"What's that?" my wife asked from near sleep in our bedroom on the second floor of the old Sears house.

"I dunno," I mumbled with disinterest.

Squeak.

"There it is again. I think something's in our room."

I pulled the cord on a swag lamp hanging above our bed.

Swoosh.

A small brown bat curved through the cold air weaving and dipping tightly as it sought escape. The door to our bedroom was closed. There was no way for the creature to exit.

"Yuck," René exclaimed as she pulled the bed covers over us. "We need to get rid of that thing," my wife observed.

"You've got to be kidding," I replied. "I'm not getting out of this bed."

My wife glared at me. I knew instantly that I'd lost the battle.

"OK, OK," I muttered. "I'll get a broom and knock the crazy thing out of the air."

Have you ever seen that old John Candy movie, *The Great Outdoors*? There's a scene where Candy and Dan Akroyd chase a wayward brown bat all over the interior of a cabin in rural Wisconsin, upsetting furniture and artifacts in the process. That's pretty much how my first experience with a bat went except that, after nearly striking my wife in the head with ill-placed blows from the broom, I realized that a tennis racket would be a better weapon. And it was.

I dispatched the little beast and we went back to sleep. We didn't have another encounter with a bat for the remainder of that night. But that doesn't mean the bats had given up trying to occupy our house.

A few weeks later, René and I took a trip to the Twin Cities. Matt stayed at my mom's. René's younger sister Colleen was recruited to stay at our house while we were away. Now, since we weren't present for the goings-on, I can't give you all the details. But it was reported to us that, as the sun set and moist autumnal fog rolled across the pasture behind the house, and as Colleen settled in for a night of television and Jiffy Pop, comfortably reclined in an overstuffed chair in our living room watching her favorite sit-com, a slight stirring of air drew her attention to the ceiling.

Above her, a pair of brown bats flitted from living room, to dining room out into the enclosed porch and back again. Colleen, being a city girl, did what any city girl would do in that situation. She screamed. Then she telephoned her dad and asked him to come out and save her from the bats. After the call, she ran out of the house, down the gravel driveway, and into the middle of the Taft Road where she waited under a cloudless fall sky, surrounded by billions of tiny stars and a near-equal number of pitching, weaving, and soaring bats, for her father.

"What was that?" René asked a week after Colleen's ill-fated stay at the house.

"Nothing," I whispered in the dark.

"I think Matt's up," she continued. "Will you go see?"

"It's nothing," I insisted.

"Mark..."

I left our warm bed and eased towards our son's bedroom. Somewhere in the bowels of the basement, the furnace kicked in. A rush of warm air pulsed through a floor vent as my bare feet moved across the carpeting. I snapped on a light in the hallway and peered into my son's bedroom. Matt was sleeping soundly.

Crash.

A *He-Man* action figure toppled from a bookshelf.

Crash.

Another figurine fell.

"What the...?" I asked.

There on the shelving, wedged between inanimate intergalactic men and women, sat an obviously confused brown bat. I exited the room taking care to shut the door behind me.

"What is it?" René asked me as I re-entered the master bedroom.

"Another bat," I replied.

"Where?"

"On Matt's bookshelf," I answered as I left the room, descended the stairway and searched for the light switch.

I rummaged through our front hall closet for the appropriate weapon. I climbed the stairs, turned on the light in Matt's room, and fixed crosshairs upon the beast's furry chest.

Thwap.

A pellet struck the animal. The critter took a header off the shelf.

"Yes," I whispered, lifting the dead rodent by its wing, the skin of the appendage no thicker than tissue paper.

Matt didn't stir. I turned out the light and retreated.

"Did you get it?" René asked as I crawled back into bed after disposing of the dead rodent.

"Yep."

"How?"

"I shot it."

"In the house? Are you crazy?"

"Nope. Just a very good shot," I replied, turning out the light.

The following evening, a family of deer mice paraded across the carpeting in front of our television set. A week later, we got our first cat.

The Ride of the Cat

I think I've written before that I'm not a huge fan of cats. Oh, I'll grant you that when you live in the country, even the most dog-loving scoundrel eventually comes to recognize that some felines, those that actually mouse, have a utilitarian value. Still, after all is said and done, cats are cats. They're not dogs, to state the obvious.

Matt, my eldest son, was just starting hockey. I was in my early thirties, still trying to reclaim, or more truthfully, find for the first time, some modicum of athletic acclaim. That year, I'd taken up both league bowling and league broomball. I didn't know it then, though I have come to realize it since, that having a child in youth hockey in Minnesota isn't being involved in a sport; it's being involved in a lifestyle. A hockey parent's personal recreational activities simply cannot be sustained in the face of that reality.

"You're gonna come with me and watch my broomball game at the Beacon. Then we'll head over to the rink for your practice."

"OK."

Matt and I were bouncing along in my metallic blue Datsun pickup truck as we spoke. I enjoyed early Saturday morning broomball games. Due to the hour, you weren't seduced into drinking beer, into being "one of the guys" and it was a good way to start the weekend. I'd played a lot of ball hockey growing up and always wanted to play ice hockey. Broomball seemed like a natural progression for a thirty-something who couldn't skate.

"How's hockey going?"

"Great. I really like my coach."

"How about your team?"

"They're OK too."

My eldest son stared out from underneath an oversized Vikings stocking cap as the little four-by-four lurched its way into Hermantown. Matt's deep brown eyes, eyes inherited from his mother, danced as he spoke. There was no question he had caught my enthusiasm for the sport of hockey. A clean white Hermantown Hawks sweatshirt covered his shoulder and elbow pads. The practice jersey hung below his waist like a nightshirt as he sat low in the bucket seat. Blue and white hockey socks, held in place by garters, concealed his shin pads and disappeared into the depths of his blue breezers. All of the equipment save the pants was brand new. The breezers were weary and tired, having been passed down from generation to generation of Hawk Squirt D players.

I drove the truck in thickly cushioned broomball shoes. The padded soles of the shoes made it difficult to feel the action of the clutch and caused me to grind the gears more than once on the trip in. A light snow fell as the truck made a left hand turn onto the Hermantown Road. The front wheels were locked in four-wheel-drive.

Matt was quiet as we pulled into the parking lot of the Beacon Inn Tavern. As I opened the driver's door, the sounds of an athletic event already in progress greeted me. Shouts of amusement, of encouragement, of disparagement, slid across the wet atmosphere, enticing me to watch the conclusion of the broomball game already in progress.

"Hurry up, Matt."

"I'm comin' as fast as I can, Dad," the child responded in a defensive tone.

I don't recall much about my game. I could make up some stuff about scoring the winning goal, having the team's only hat trick, or the like. But truthfully, after so many years, the games I played that year have merged into one memory.

What I do remember about that Saturday is the cat.

From time to time on the farm, we had cats. Generally, they'd come and go as they pleased, living quite contently in our garage or in the old barn. I'd have to remind the kids, at that time, Matt, later, both Dylan and Chris as they grew into the job, to change the kitty litter and feed the animals. But in truth, cats are a lot less effort than dogs. That's probably why they give you a lot less in return. There's really no obligation placed upon them because their owners don't have to do all that much for them.

Contrast that with dogs, where you have to train them not to crap in the house, not to tear up the garden, not to eat children's winter boots. In return for all that attention, dogs give back a certain amount of affection. Not so with cats.

When the broomball game was over, we had time to kill. Matt sipped a Coke and I had a cup of coffee while reliving the excitement of the contest with my teammates. There was no reason to rush. My son's hockey practice didn't start until noon.

At the time, we had a cat; a yellow striped tabby named Snickers. Admittedly, Snickers was one of the better cats we owned over the years. He was friendly to the point of being nearly canine. He stayed out of trouble and kept out of my hair, which endeared the creature to me.

As Matt and I walked across the frozen gravel of the Beacon Inn parking lot, I heard the faint cry of a cat. Nothing really unusual about that in Hermantown, a rural town with probably hundreds, if not thousands, of cats living within its borders. But the tenor of the call seemed vaguely familiar.

Meow.

The cry grew louder as we approached the Datsun. It wouldn't have been surprising to find a stray cat, or even a cat that lived at the bar, seeking shelter beneath the chassis of a truck parked in a tavern's parking lot.

"Where's that coming from?" Matt asked.

"I think it's coming from under the truck."

"It sounds like Snickers."

"Matt, all cats sound the same."

"Uh uh. I can tell Snicker's meow."

Dubious, I knelt to the ground and searched under my truck for the source of the sound.

Meow.

"I'm sure that's Snickers."

Opening the driver's door, I pulled vigorously on the hood release. Metal creaked loudly in the cool air as the cable securing the latch relaxed.

Meow.

I walked to the front of the Datsun. My gloved hands found another lever. Metal creaked as a second latch released. Standing over the engine compartment in my perspiration-soaked sweat pants and broomball jersey, "Radford and Company" stenciled across the chest, I raised the hood.

There, perched comfortably on the cold four-cylinder engine, was Snickers. Other than a little grease and oil on his normally pristine fur, the cat appeared none the worse from his twenty mile ride into Hermantown.

The Hockey Stick

My eldest son Matt hasn't worn goalie pads in years. Before his playing days ended, my wife René and I watched him play ice hockey from the time he was six until his sophomore year in high school. There were so many games, so many road trips and tournaments over that span of time, that I don't remember many details about his career. But I do remember the names and faces of the little boys and girls he played with.

There are objects I've held onto over the years from Matt's days on ice: team photographs, videotapes of games, snapshots from tournament trips with other parents and their families and the like. And then there is the miniature hockey stick.

It's about eighteen inches long and made of maple. "Cooper"- the name of a Canadian hockey equipment manufacturer- is stenciled in black across the flat surface of the stick's handle. Someone, a coach, the team mom, or the team manager colored in a blue ring around the stick's handle, down where the blade meets the shaft and added "Squirt C 1988-1989" in the same ink.

I keep the stick in my office to remind me of simpler days, of more innocent times. The stick represents Matt's last year as a true Squirt (today I think they call that level "Mites" instead of Squirt C), the last year of total enjoyment of the fastest game on ice. The next year, and each year thereafter until his career ended, Matt faced tryouts and the prospect of "cuts": designations made by a panel of hockey coaches as to which level he'd play at. It's too bad I didn't understand what the future held in store that last year of Squirt C's. I think I would have relished the season even more.

Youth athletics isn't just an opportunity for kids to make friends, learn a sport, and begin realizing that life involves competition; wins and losses, ups and downs. It's also an opportunity for the parents to learn a few things as well.

That year, our little team was coached by a guy I had, and still have, a great deal of respect for. Tim has a hockey background but that isn't what made him a good coach. He has unflappable patience, a keen interest in the welfare of his little charges, and a steady hand with discipline. His son played on the team, a big, smiling kid with a wonderful sense of humor and a love of good-natured competition. The kid signed my little replica stick as did ten other boys. I happen to have their autographs because I was an assistant coach that year.

It was an intense game, at least in my mind. In truth, I was so wound up watching my kid that I really shouldn't have been on the bench.

"Come on guys," I yelled at the top of my lungs. "Move your feet."

Jeff, the other assistant coach and I worked the doors of the team bench and shouted encouragement to the kids. Tim stood quietly a distance away from us surveying the play.

"Brian, get the lead out," Jeff shouted as his son lagged behind the rest of the Hawk forwards down the ice. Jeff's kid was little, fast, and had a good eye for the net.

"Yeah, Matt. Get up there and help out your team."

Matt turned and gave me look of disdain as he coasted by the bench. He was a forward. We called him the "Junkyard Dog" because he liked to park himself in front of the opposing net and slam the puck home. It was less work that way. Why waste all your energy carrying the puck up ice when someone else can do it for you?

I don't recall the score of the game. I know we were at home, in the Hermantown Arena, playing a regular season game. I also seem to recall that it was a close contest, requiring extensive vocal intervention from Jeff and me to spur on our kids.

"What the heck is wrong with you, Ref?" I called out in a belligerent tone when an official missed an easy off-sides call against our opponent. My face was likely red, my testosterone rushing, as I became more and more heated.

That's when Tim took me aside.

"Mark. What do you think you're doing?" Tim asked in a subdued voice. He called me over to where he was perched on the back of the bench. His head was bent forward so he could talk quietly, so that no one else could hear our conversation.

"That guy blew it. They got a goal off that piece of garbage," I whispered.

"Number one, it wasn't that bad a call. I've made worse," Tim interjected. "And number two, you're a coach. You're wearing a blue jacket with the words "Hermantown Hawks" on it. What kind of example do you think you're setting for these young men?"

A huge lump formed in my throat. Tim was right. I was acting like one of the hockey parents that I'd always vowed I'd never emulate. I sheepishly looked away from the coach and pondered a response. Jeff stayed a considerable distance from us, unwilling to become a target of a similar lecture.

I study the names on the hockey stick sitting on my desk in the St. Louis County Courthouse. Four of the boys whose names appear on the stick went on to play in the Minnesota State High School Hockey Tournament. One kid played in two state tournaments as a goalie. Another never played high school hockey but went to state in track. Justin, one of two kids on the team to battle cancer, became a 1,000 yard rusher in his senior year in football.

Five of the boys, including my own son, went to college on the strength of their minds, not their bodies. In fact, David, a member of that collegiate group, graduated at the top of his high school class. And two of the players from that Squirt C team, maybe more, have given something back to the sport by becoming youth coaches, by putting themselves on the line as role models for younger kids.

The names on that little stick bring to mind distant events; some sad, some tragic. Less than perfect memories reinforce the notion that not every kid who excels in a sport lives long enough to realize his or her potential.

But there is one signature that stands out whenever I consider the names inscribed on that piece of maple. And when I scrutinize the gently crafted letters left behind by the coach's son, young man who died far too early, Tim's admonition rings as true today as it did years ago:

"Mark, try and remember that this isn't real life. These are just little kids trying to play a game."

Dylan's Shack

Sometimes my ideas are hair-brained. Still, despite my best attempts at self-sabotage, things usually work out. Take, for instance, the day I decided to build Dylan, my second son, a shack. Well, not really build him one. My carpentry skills are too meager for that. Relocate would be a better description.

When we first moved onto the old Drew Place, the hobby farm we bought in 1984 out in Fredenberg Township north of Duluth, there were six structures on seven and a half acres. There was the house: A Sears prefabricated home delivered in crates to the site along the banks of the Cloquet River back in 1921 by draft horse and wagon. There was the original dairy barn; a chicken coop; a pump house; an old garage absent doors, windows, and shingles; and a newer four-car garage. As time passed, I dismantled the old garage and used the salvaged boards for other projects. And before the old barn and chicken coop were burned to the ground as training exercises for our local volunteer fire department, I got the bright notion that the pump house would make a good shack for Dylan.

 The building at issue is approximately eight feet by six feet and six feet tall to the rafters. Just big enough for a card table, a couple of chairs, and a set of built-in bunk beds attached to the far wall. When the idea to relocate the structure first popped into my head, the shed's roofing was nearly gone. The siding was painted a hideous shade of blue that didn't match the color of the other buildings on our property. The floor was hastily mixed asphalt that heaved every spring so that the door, a door I'd retrieved from the local landfill, wouldn't open from about March 15th until June 1st.

 Despite the building's shortcomings, René had adopted the shed as her gardening depot. We hung our rakes, shovels, and assorted other implements on hooks in the building. I'd constructed shelves and we'd filled them with gardening tools, fertilizer, seeds, and the like. The building was functional if unattractive. But the chicken coop, until we burned it down and built a new pole building, was ample enough to accept the items formerly kept in the pump house. And so, my plans to move the shed were implemented.

"Larry," I said one summer evening, "I need your advice."

I was talking on the telephone to my close friend, a former carpenter, now fire fighter.

"How's that?" Larry asked.

"I want to move the old pump house across Knudsen Creek, put it by the Norway pines along the stream so Dylan has a place to call his own," I said.

"Uh huh."

"How would one go about picking up something like that and moving it?" I asked coyly, fearful that Larry might sense the barbs of a hook sinking into his mouth.

"Mmm," my pal said, mulling over how deeply he wanted to commit himself to my project. "How big is it?"

I described the shed.

"You could jack it up and move it with my snowmobile trailer," Larry offered.

"A half-day's work?"

"Sounds about right."

There was a pause. Larry knew what was coming next. He'd dealt with his carpentry-impaired pal too many times. I'd worked as a construction laborer with Larry back when I was in college. On the job site, I was never allowed to use tools. Tools are dangerous in my hands. Well, I take that back. The boss of the construction outfit let me use a shovel. But only with supervision.

"Larry, I don't suppose you'd have some free time to lend your old friend a hand?"

It was Larry's turn to pause.

"I've got a few days off next week," he finally submitted. "What're we gonna pull it with?"

"I've got a hitch on my International," I advised, referring to my Model 606 utility tractor.

"That'll work."

By the time Larry sawed through all of the wall joists sunk deep into the asphalt floor, by the time we'd raised the bulk of the building off the ground, elevating it with four large jacks so that Larry's trailer could be backed under the shed, an entire day had passed.

It was dusk when I put my International 606 in gear and began to pull the shed towards Knudsen Creek. The axle of the trailer bowed. It was clear that the weight on the snowmobile trailer far exceeded any manufacturer's recommendations. Larry, my buddy Eddie (another fireman and a good friend), and I held our collective breath as the wheels on the trailer turned. The axles groaned but the trailer remained intact.

Catastrophe nearly struck when we climbed a small rise and the weight of the shed shifted, causing the hydraulics leveling the trailer hitch to rise precariously. Eddie and Larry intervened. The combined weight of my two pals standing on the trailer tongue defeated gravity. What can I say? Firemen are well fed.

After unloading the shed at the building site, it remained suspended on timbers for a week while I constructed a new plywood floor. Once the floor was complete, I lowered the structure into place with the jacks and secured the floor to the frame. Dylan and I then painted the exterior walls with white latex. I added a screen door and covered the wall studs with cheap chipboard and built two small bunk beds into the rear wall. When I was finished, despite my meager skills, the place wasn't half bad.

The relocation of the pump house started a new tradition. Beginning in fourth or fifth grade, and continuing every year until high school, Dylan invited a select group of buddies to stay overnight in the shack after the last day of school. My wife René and I supplied the soda pop, hot dogs, chips, and makings for s'mores. We also monitored the festivities from a distance.

Year after year, the boys stayed up late watching the embers of a campfire, playing youthful games of tag, hide-and-seek, and capture the flag long into the night. At times, they took excursions to visit the abandoned cabins at the end of Knudsen Road, all the while listening to tales of murder and mayhem centered on a mythical old man who butchered the children of Fredenberg. Dylan's invented legend still lives on in the form of a trail sign on one of my cross-country ski trails located on our property:

Old Man Farley's Trail.

The ultimate highlight of these gatherings was the ceremonial burning of homework brought by the boys, by Jake, Ian, Ben, Brandon, Frankie, Cory, and a handful of others who stayed overnight at the shack after the last day of school. Never having been invited to witness the boys' celebration, I can only imagine the theology their festivities involved. I am certain that, unlike Lenten and Good Friday services observed by Christians, where the pallor of death and suffering compels solemnity, the boys' celebrations centered upon joy, the joy of watching their homework burn. More than this, I cannot say.

Things, of course, change. Dylan and his pals outgrew the shack. Girls, not ghost stories, became the primary focus of late night conversations. Jake's family moved a little ways down Arrowhead Road in Hermantown. Their new home came equipped with a guest cottage. This cottage, which became, by default, "The Shack", has a loft, electricity, and heat. Girls were close by. The boys could listen to "tunes".

A final end-of-the-school-year- gathering on our place occurred at the conclusion of my son's ninth grade year. The boys had grown too large to fit comfortably in the old pump house. Dylan borrowed our family tent and pitched it alongside the Cloquet River for the event. The boys' camped near the disintegrating cabin Dylan claims was once home to Old Man Farley.

At least not every dream of youth is forgotten.

Beware of Toxic Tuesday

In September of 1990, I was in the process of recovering from back surgery when my wife conceived the big idea that I should write the Great American Novel. When my wounds healed sufficiently to allow me to take long walks, I started to daydream. Plot themes and imaginary characters sprang to life during these sojourns.

Winter came. My walks gave way to swimming in a local pool. As I increased my time in the water, I mentally re-worked an emerging story. Late at night, in the quiet of our eighty-five year old farmhouse, I laboriously transferred words from yellow legal pads into our old Tandy computer's memory.

On Christmas of that year, René gave me Jeff Herman's book, *Writer's Guide to Book Editors, Publishers and Literary Agents*. I was heartened that my better half thought enough of my writing to steer me towards publication. Thoughts of life as a famous writer began to seduce me. I was tired of being a trial lawyer. Writing looked to be a way out. John Grisham was a lawyer once, wasn't he? So were Scott Turow and Barry Reed.

I put Herman's volume on the shelf. I was not ready to market my book. I knew that my manuscript, *November One*, would require months to complete. But life got in the way of writing. Daily tasks made the moments available to work on the book scarce. Another winter was upon me before the novel was ready for professional scrutiny. I pulled Herman's tome from its resting-place and jotted down the names and addresses of literary agents who seemed appropriate for my book. I began to send query letters to these agents in batches of five letters at a time.

On May 5, 1992, the first query letters were mailed. Within days, I heard back from the queried agents. All declined to take a look at my work. I struggled to understand why no one thought my manuscript was worthy of at least a cursory read.

On May 20th- five new names were added to my list of potential agents. Though three agencies responded with resounding "no thanks", their rejection letters were at least polite. I never heard back from the other two. Self-doubt began to cloud my good humor. But on May 28, 1992, jubilation! Ms. Roslyn Targ asked for the first 50 pages of my manuscript. I sent the requested excerpt the next day. By June 10, I was reading the following:

I have now had an opportunity to read your manuscript and unfortunately I do not feel enthusiastic enough to take on its representation. Hopefully another agent will feel otherwise.

Good luck,

R. Targ.

My tenacity as a civil trial attorney compelled me to keep trying. Natasha Kern, Ruth Wreschner, Judith Berg (remember that name, you'll see it later on) and two other noted agents were targeted. My attitude improved considerably when I received word that both Ms. Kern and Ms. Wreschner wanted to read portions of the manuscript.

A few weeks later, I was reading the following:

I have the feeling that you are a very nice person and probably also a good lawyer, just the person I would love to number among my clients...

I sensed such an introduction could only be followed by a big fat "but..."

Ms. Wreschner was kind but unimpressed:

Do ask another agent since opinions differ but I don't think I would be successful for you. It might also help to read some books on fiction writing... or take some fiction writing courses. Best of luck to you. If your book gets published, I'll be the loser!

In retrospect, my sensitivity was misplaced. My writing needed guidance. However, with thoughts of "Book of the Month Club" fame dancing before me, an agent's scathing critique of my literary abilities was the last thing I wanted to acknowledge.

A week later, I was on top of the world again.

"Mark," my wife yelled to me as I was tilling our vegetable garden, "there's a Ms. Kern on the telephone for you."

41

"Hello," I offered when I picked up the telephone receiver. "This is Mark."

"Mr. Munger, Natasha Kern. I've read the first few chapters of your book. While the writing needs some work, I like the plot. I want you to consider working with an editor to smooth out the rough edges. They charge by the page but I think that it would be worth a try. If you like, I can send you a list of reputable editors and you can pick the one you want to work with," she said.

Ms. Kern laid it on the line. There were some problems, yes. But they could be overcome.

"I'm willing to give it a try," I responded meekly.

"I want to see the finished product," Ms. Kern added.

Natasha sent me a list of editors. I selected Ms. Leslie Payne to work with. I wrote to Ms. Payne. She called me back. We came to an agreement. It looked like things were finally going my way.

The citizenry of Duluth, Minnesota (my home) will always remember June 30, 1992 as "Toxic Tuesday". On that date, a Burlington Northern freight train derailed, sending a tanker full of benzene into the Nemadji River. The mixture of benzene and water created a poisonous cloud. I was one of tens of thousands of Duluthians who scurried out of town as part of a mass evacuation of the Twin Ports of Duluth and Superior, Wisconsin.

June 30, 1992 stands out for me personally, not because of my escape from benzene hell, but because of another telephone call I received.

"Mark, there's someone on the phone calling about your book," René related as I filled our riding lawn mower with gasoline.

Once again I went inside the house to talk to a stranger over the telephone about my novel.

"Mr. Munger, Brice Harding from the Judith Berg Agency. Ms. Berg asked that I give you a call. We're interested in your book."

There it was. Further confirmation that what I had written was worthy of consideration. Two days later, I received the Berg Agency's submission guidelines. Within the week, the first 100 pages of *November One* were en route to Ms. Berg. I felt caught in a heady whirlwind of excitement. Two agents wanted my work! I had two professionals ready, willing, and able to go to war in the trenches of the New York publishing industry on my behalf.

On September 2, I called Judith Berg. The agent made it clear that she wanted to represent *November One*.

"René," I said to my wife as we sat on a swing on the front porch of our farmhouse sometime after I spoke with Ms. Berg, "I don't know what to do. Natasha Kern thinks that the book has merit but wants me to work with an editor."

"Uh huh," my wife responded.

"On the other hand, Ms. Berg will take the book as is."

"Sounds like you have a decision to make," my wife said.

A few days later, I signed a contract with Ms. Berg. I was feeling on top of the world.

By January of 1993, my Ms. Berg was satisfied that the book had reached a sufficient level of integrity to submit it to prospective publishers. I began to receive memoranda from the agency listing the names of publishers being provided with *November One*. That same month I also received a contract from my agent regarding the potential sale of the electronic rights of my book. I was on a roll. Just a few short months after entering into the publishing arena, people were lining up to offer me contracts. I signed and returned the E-rights agreement as fast as I could.

By early June, all of the publishers contacted by Ms. Berg had rejected *November One*. Confused, I wrote to Judith (we were on a first name basis by then). I implored her to advise me whether (as others had opined) the book needed major rehabilitation. I received no response to my letter.

A year passed. By March of 1994, I was getting concerned that Ms. Berg and I were "barking up the wrong tree". I again asked for any comments or concerns that the agency (or any of the contacted publishers) might have regarding the manuscript. The agent provided a rejection letter from Tor books:

Although the subject matter intrigued me and the plot maintained my interest, I found the writing to be slightly awkward at times. Often, the dialogue was forced and unnatural. Therefore, I'm going to pass on this one.

(Letter from N. Montemarano of Tor Books dated 5/12/93).

Mr. Montemarano's comments were startling. I began to believe that the other agent's observations about *November One* were likely to have been on the mark. I called the agency and set up an appointment to speak with Ms. Berg. We talked. I stayed put. She was confident a publisher would be found.

On October 19, 1994, I received a proposed contract from Northwest Publishing (NPI) in Utah. My agent's cover letter indicated that, while she was unable to obtain an advance from NPI for my work, she had negotiated an agreement on my behalf:

However, I did speak with acquisitions and with publishing regarding the value of your book and we were able to negotiate some cooperative terms.

(Letter of 10/19/94)

I'm a lawyer. I'm able to understand legalese. As I read through the proposed agreement, I noted that I was expected to "front" NPI the sum of $6,125.00. Even though I was new to the book publishing world, the proposal sounded an awful lot like vanity publishing, something I was not interested in.

I called my agent. I had a number of questions, not the least of which was: "Is NPI a reputable company?"

Ms. Berg assured me that NPI was a solvent regional publisher marketing 100-150 titles per year through industry giants Barnes and Noble, and Baker and Taylor. After our conversation, I felt immeasurably better. I was convinced that "cooperative publishing", where NPI agreed to pay the majority of the cost associated with printing 10,000 copies of the book in trade paperback and agreed to provide nationwide marketing support, was not such a bad deal after all. On December 2, 1994, I received an amended agreement directly from Mr. James Van Treese, the owner of NPI. My cash contribution to the cooperative effort had been reduced to

$3,062.50. All of the other terms and conditions of the deal remained in place. Enthused by the notion that my long path towards literary glamour was but a few short steps away, I implored my wife to let me send Mr. Van Treese a check.

"Look at it this way," I argued. "If everything goes sour, we're only out a few thousand bucks."

Confident that NPI would deliver the goods, having been assured as to the publisher's reputation, and having been provided with a copy of NPI's catalog (as well as a sample of one of their books), I convinced my wife to let me send the cash.

A month later, I received a publication schedule from NPI. In July of 1995, Mr. Van Treese requested a three-month extension of the book's release date. I agreed to the modification at the behest of my agent.

September 1995. Ms. Berg wrote and explained that Mr. Van Treese was seeking an additional extension. The language of the letter caught my attention:

Should Mr. Van Treese/NPI fail to publish according to the schedule and fail to return your money, we will discuss a legal recourse at that time. It is my hope that I am just being an alarmist... but I feel it's best to be
prepared in the event that NPI defaults.

(Letter of 9/22/95).

I sensed trouble. Embarrassed, I said nothing to my wife. It became more difficult to fend off the inquiries of friends, family, and neighbors regarding the book.

"How's your novel coming?" my friend Jan asked whenever she saw me.

"Slowly," was my patterned response.

An edited galley of the book arrived in March of 1996. I supplied NPI with revisions and a color photograph taken by my wife, an artist, which seemed perfect for the book's cover. I convinced myself that Ms. Berg had sounded a false alarm until NPI sent me the following handwritten note:

Enclosed is a copy of what the art director has come up with despite the situation here at Northwest. At this time, I don't know how long this will take to be printed. If you have any questions

45

concerning this copy, or if I can be of any further help at this time, please call me at...

The note wasn't written on NPI stationary. I tried to call NPI. The company's toll free number had been disconnected. I dialed direct. I was told by the person who answered that the publisher had filed for bankruptcy. I dialed my agent and left several intense messages for Ms. Berg. She didn't return my calls.

As I clung to shreds of faith that NPI would come back into the picture, I began to receive legal papers from the bankruptcy court and my greatest fears were confirmed:

The trustee filed a complaint against James Van Treese and Jason Van Treese on February 13, 1997. The complaint seeks recovery from these two individuals of at least $10,500,000.00 based upon defendants' corporate mismanagement of NPI...

(Court Notice dated 4/14/97)

As Paul Simon said, I felt everything "slip-sliding away." NPI still held the corrected galleys, the computer disks, and my wife's original photograph for the book's cover. I, along with many others who had been bilked, hired a third party service to scour NPI's files in hopes of salvaging my intellectual property. The service was unable to retrieve anything from NPI related to my book.

Disgruntled but undeterred, I pressed onward. Ms. Berg lined up another publisher, Caramoor Press. Exhausted by the NPI debacle, I agreed to work with Caramoor. I began to rewrite my novel for the 14th or 15th time, relieved that I wasn't expected to send Caramoor any money. Shortly after signing a contract with Caramoor, I received a gushing letter from Ms. Berg:

Congratulations on your publishing contract with Caramoor. They have informed me that they will soon be able to announce your release date.

(Letter of 3/19/97).

Nearly five years after my first contact with the Berg Agency, things seemed poised to come to some sort of conclusion. Whether I became rich, famous, or critically acclaimed mattered little. Positive closure for my work, for my sweat and toil, was all that mattered by that point.

Two weeks later I received an envelope from my agent. The letter inside contained this bit of "bad news":

We are now at the point where we are diligently trying to sever all ties with Caramoor...We have requested that all materials belonging to our clients are returned to our office by April 9, 1997...

(Letter of 4/4/97)

My agent went on to urge "us" (this was a form letter) to consider publishing with "Romantic Press", a publishing venture Ms. Berg was just beginning. Enraged at being duped again, I detailed my frustrations to the Berg Agency in a letter:

It has been five years since I was first contacted by you regarding the novel and I am in exactly the same situation today as I was then with several major exceptions:

1. *I have lost $3,500.00, give or take a few pennies on the NPI fiasco;*

2. *I have lost five years of time;*

3. *Your agency has presented the work to scores of potential publishers... to no avail, obviously diminishing the chances that I will be able to find another agent to take on the work.*

(Letter dated 7/15/97)

A few months later, I finally terminated my contract with my agent.

To make my embarrassment more palpable, a reporter from a Salt Lake City newspaper requested an interview with me about my dealings with NPI. What could I tell her? That I was greedy for fame? That I was, despite twenty years of formal education, undeniably stupid? After taking a deep breath, I called her back. A few days later, she sent me a copy of the article she'd written. Thankfully, the story didn't mention me by name.

Am I bitter about my fate? I don't think so. During my long and difficult education regarding the world of publishing and literary agents, I came to the realization that my first novel needed help. I hadn't paid my dues. Once I came to this point of recognition, I took a few steps back.

During the winter of 1997 I began to write a weekly essay column for our local paper. Years of receiving personal, heart-warming accolades from readers of those articles have convinced me that I can write. I just needed to find my own voice, my own style. Learning a subject, whether it's law or art, requires study. I've become an enthusiastic reader of *Poets and Writers, Glimmer Train, Grain, Heron Dance, Writer's Journal,* and other literary periodicals in the hopes that I can gain an informal education in the craft of writing.

These days, whenever I have a block of free time, I work on short stories and essays, mailing two or three pieces a season to literary magazines, ever hopeful that my writing strikes a chord. And I spend hours reading the stuff I should have read twenty-five years ago in college: Hemingway, Faulkner, O'Connor, Lawrence, Steinbeck.

Who knows? Someday, I might attend a writing workshop or take a stab at writing another novel.

Note: The names associated with the agency which represented me are fictional. The rest, as they say, is nothing but fact.

POSTSCRIPT:

In October of 2000 *November One* was re-titled **The Legacy,** published by Savage Press of Superior, Wisconsin, became a regional bestseller, and remains in print through Cloquet River Press. The book was acclaimed by *The Mystery Review Quarterly* (Summer 2001) as a "marvelous first novel."

Leaving Mayo

I shouldn't be here. My wife is eight and a half months pregnant. I still owe American Express two thousand dollars for a trip to San Francisco I gave my wife for her fortieth birthday. I don't have cancer and I don't think I'm dying, at least not any faster than I should be.

For seven years I've had a mystery disease. Disease is maybe a little strong. A disease is something defined, found, maybe incurable, but at least known. What I have, no one seems to be able to categorize. I guess it can't be called a disease. I really can't even call it a condition. Might be able to call it a condition if someone could figure out just what it is.

I know it is foolish to envy people with tragic illnesses. I know that, given the slow advance of my symptoms, chances are that whatever I have will not kill me in the immediate future. Maybe that's why I hate being here, being at the Mayo Clinic. I just don't fit in. Everyone else here seems to have a condition or a disease that has a name, a treatment. I have symptoms. Ten years' worth of symptoms. Joint pain. Mouth ulcers. Bleeding. Stomach upsets. Inability to sleep. Fatigue. Pain in my eyes that feels like someone actually poured sand in them while I sleep at night. Slightly elevated CPKs, Sed rates, CRPs, Bilirubin. Interesting observations and minor alterations in my body's chemistry. But nothing significant enough or helpful enough to allow any of the twenty or so physicians I've seen to provide me with a diagnosis, let alone a course of treatment.

"How's your stress level?" I've been asked by each of them.

"Fine," I say, "except for the fact I have all these things going on with my forty-three year old body and no one can figure out what the hell is wrong with me."

I get up at four thirty in the morning to drive from Duluth to Rochester. The first time down here, in 1992, I drove. My second visit, in 1994, I took a plane. I'm back to driving.

49

I park in one of the downtown ramps and walk the two blocks to the Mayo Building. A heavy fog disguises the upper-most floors of the Clinic. A bronze statue of a naked guy, his balls shriveled in the cold, his skin turned a nasty green by weather, is fastened to the marble exterior of the building. He's perched directly over the main entrance. I look across the street, trying to see if my church, the Episcopal Church, is still there. It is. Somehow knowing my religion is nearby props me up as I enter the Mayo building.

I'm late. I was supposed to be here at 8:30 am to register. It's 9:15am. I run excuses over and over in my brain.

I'm sorry I'm late. My wife is expecting and she had false labor.

A lie but at least one based upon fact. After all, my wife is ready to give birth.

I had a flat up near St. Paul.

Another lie with absolutely no basis in reality.

My back was acting up so I pulled over at Hinckley and walked around.

Two parts of this story are true. My back, actually my left hip, is aching. It went out on me, as my joints sometimes do, without any reason, three days ago. I've iced it, pain killered-it, rested it, and put heat on it. I walk with a noticeable limp because of it. And I did get out in Hinckley to use the john. But I'm not late because of it.

I'm late because I thought Interstate 35 went to Rochester, Minnesota, when in fact, it does not. It goes to Albert Lea. And then to Iowa.

"Hi, Mr. Munger. Have a seat. The doctor will be right with you," the receptionist says between smiles. She takes papers from me and never asks why I'm late. I limp to a padded chair in the immense lobby on the fifteenth floor and wait my turn.

I spend an hour with a rheumatologist, a guy with a slight foreign accent. Italian or Spanish, I think. He seems to be about my age. He knows little about my problem, or at least that's what I perceive. He has less than half an inch of my doctor's chart from Duluth. I know the complete chart is more like six inches of narrative and test results.

50

I want to ask him why it is that doctors can get by reading only part of a patient's file when an attorney, at least any good attorney, feels compelled to read all of a client's file. But I don't ask. I'm hoping this guy has something new to add, some new approach to help me understand why I feel the way I do. Why I can't play softball anymore. Why I bleed into the toilet. Why I'm so tired, despite eight hours of sleep, that I can barely see straight.

He asks the same questions I've been asked twenty or thirty times by other physicians. I try to give the same answers. He zeros in on a previous diagnosis made by one of his partners at Mayo.

"I see here that Dr. Marx thought you had Fibromyalgia when he saw you in 1994. Do your remember that?"

I try not to sound perturbed. I nod my head.

"Yes, I remember that," I remark quietly. "But given my history since then, the doctors in Duluth don't think that fits what's going on."

He nods. I think I've steered him off that path. I want to. I know from my personal injury practice that patients are given the diagnosis of "Fibromyalgia", muscle pain of unknown etiology or origin, as a diagnosis of last resort. It isn't a disease. It is a description conveniently used to label a cluster of symptoms.

We talk more. He examines me. He pushes and prods each sector of my body. Some of my joints are tender. When his fingers probe my left hip, I double in pain. He motions for me to sit on the couch.

"From the looks of things, I'd say we're dealing with Fibromyalgia. I'll run some more tests, most of the things you've had before, blood, urine, stool, colonoscopy. But it sure looks like Fibromyalgia to me."

I want to scream. I want to tell him:

Don't dump a label on my condition simply so you can push me back out the door. Dig, damn it. Dig deeper into your bag of tests and tricks and medicines and find out what the hell is wrong with me.

But I don't. I sit quietly, listening.

51

"I'll be right back. Dr. Jones wants to look in on you. Don't get dressed yet."

He leaves me in the cold, vacant exam room. There is nothing to entertain me in the room except portions of my own medical chart, which I've read and re-read before.

My hip and lower back begin to burn. I stand up and walk over to the mirror. I look at my body. There is more hair on my chest than I remember. Up until my mid-thirties, my chest was essentially hairless. Now there are curls and wisps of dark black hair up and down my chest, all the way to my navel and below. Here and there, a white hair signals my age. I touch the scars on my belly where my gall bladder was removed three years ago. The damn thing didn't have stones. It just stopped doing what it was supposed to do. Luckily, I was able to have it pulled out through a scope. All that remains of the pain are three small scars, each less than a half-inch long.

My right thigh sports a two inch scar, the result of a deep muscle biopsy. The biopsy revealed nothing but left me with the scar as a nice reminder of medical futility.

"It'll hurt for a day or so. Nothing major. Just don't try to roller blade the next day," a nameless, faceless doctor had cautioned before sending me for the biopsy.

Yeah, right. The doctor that fed me that line was a liar. Or had never bothered to ask one of his patients what the biopsy site felt like for the next week. I'm not a baby. I ran two marathons, made it through Marine Corps and Army basic training. After the muscle biopsy, I couldn't walk for a week.

I finger a thick scar on my lower back. It runs from just above the belt line to my butt. Somewhere along the way, I had a low-back fusion. They took out a piece of my hipbone and inserted it between the vertebrae in the spine to stop forward slippage in my lumbar spine. Christian, my third, used to examine the scar when he scratched my back. Maybe he'll be a surgeon someday.

Looking into the mirror, I pat my gut. I'm happy that when the nurse weighed me I'd lost five pounds. And somehow gained 3/4". I've always been five ten. Today I was just a tad under five eleven. Maybe I'll eventually be tall enough to jam a basketball.

I don't like the roll of fat that has crept around my middle. I work hard to keep it off, exercising three or four times a week. But the fatigue makes me pace my exercise. It's tough to work out more than a half-hour at a time. Still, overall, the picture I see isn't as bad as it could be.

Dr. Jones surprises me as I'm looking at myself in the glass. He sits down next to me on the couch. He's in a suit. I'm in my briefs. The other guy stands by the window and doesn't say anything. Jones looks younger than I am. I like him. He says things that I want to hear.

"What's the worst problem confronting you right now, in terms of symptoms?" he asks in a genuine voice. Of course, the voice could simply be very well practiced. I accept it as sincere.

"The eye pain and the fatigue. I'm a lawyer and a writer. I can live with bleeding. I know it isn't going to kill me. I can live with joint pain. Hell, I've had a back fusion for worse pain than what I'm dealing with now."

"Makes sense. Tell you what. Let's do some more blood work, repeat some things. There are a few autoimmune problems that I can rule out. Lupus is one. You don't have it. But there are others that involve the joints and the digestive tract. They might be more in tune with what's going on. Sound reasonable?"

"I gotta tell you that the word that comes to mind here, doc, is frustrating."

I try to be as candid with him as I can. I sense he wants honesty and that he will return it to me.

"I understand. We'll see what we can put together. Get dressed. Someone will come by with your schedule."

I've been through this part of the routine before. I've taken off three days from work to allow for the extensive work-up that Mayo prides itself on. I also know that, for whatever reason, there is no way the testing and exams will ever be completed in three days. When I get the documents from the front desk, they have me staying in Rochester for five days. I can't afford it. I have a baby on the way. I don't

53

share any of this with the scheduling lady. I simply tell her I have to be back to work in three days.

"I'll see what I can do," she says as she hands me a small folder with seven or eight appointment sheets placed inside it in chronological order.

"Keep these for now. Go to the ones you can. I'll start working on getting the others changed."

"Thanks," I mumble.

Staring at the papers, knowing that they represent several thousands of dollars of sophisticated medical care, I'm thankful that I've used up the deductible on my health insurance. I wonder to myself what I would do if I didn't have insurance through work.

I'd live with it, I tell myself. *I sure as hell wouldn't be here.*

I begin my parade through Mayo's diagnostic maze. I start with a simple blood test. I take the elevator to the basement, the Subway level of the Clinic. I hand my paperwork to another lady behind another counter and take a seat. I sit a row or two away from two women. One of the women appears to be about fifty, the other, about twenty-five.

"She told me I have to make up my mind today. If both lumps are malignant, she recommends a mastectomy with an immediate implant. If one is benign and one malignant, I have the option of a lumpectomy, though the scarring might be pretty bad."

The older woman is speaking very loudly. It is obvious she is anxious. She should be. She has cancer. She has a diagnosis. And it isn't good. I realize I shouldn't be here. I don't have a diagnosis. I don't have a condition, at least one that warrants me wasting the time of the Mayo Clinic. She does. If she doesn't get help, she'll die. If I don't get help, I'll simply grow tired and shit a little more blood. I don't belong here.

"I thought the doctor said you needed radiation," the younger woman whispers.

"That's only if I go with the lumpectomy. If I go with the mastectomy, then I don't need it."

"What about chemotherapy?" her daughter asks.

"Only if the lymph nodes are involved. But the problem is, I'll be out. I need to decide now, before she goes in, whether I want the mastectomy or the lumpectomy. What should I do?"

I think about the woman and the terrible choice she is presented. Without knowing the true nature of her condition, she must decide a course of action from which she cannot retreat. Before I can settle the issue in my own mind, my name is called. I wander off for what is likely my fiftieth blood test in the past ten years.

I do my business. I leave urine and stool samples in containers provided to me by the Clinic on stainless steel carts parked at intervals on the lower level. As I walk through the tiled corridors of the Clinic, I pass Moslems, Pakistanis, Hindus, Blacks, Asians; a myriad of races and cultures that we never see in my hometown. None of these people are poor. They are foreigners with means. They have come here, to the Mecca of Medicine, seeking a cure for whatever ails them.

The Moslem women, their faces tightly wrapped with gauze, provoke my curiosity. Don't they know that this is America? Don't they know they can rip the fabric from their faces and be free of the oppression of their culture? I realize my chauvinism just as I think it. I remember that our culture is not universal. I walk on.

I pass wheelchair after wheelchair of deserted, pathetic people, their absent eyes staring into space. These people do not seem to know where they are. Maybe it's better that way. Will they die here? That's doubtful. They'll likely make it to rest homes, where they will resume staring until they die. I leave the Clinic and walk outside towards my hotel.

An old man in a wheelchair gets on the elevator at the Kahler Hotel with me. His attendant, a middle aged African-American woman, smiles widely, exposing beautiful white teeth. The patient has only one leg. A bandaged stump is all that remains of his other lower appendage. I try not to stare at the stump. I try not to wonder how he lost his leg. It could have been diabetes or a farming accident. It's none of my damn business.

55

In the quiet of my hotel room I open the packet of appointments and study them. I've been through each test before. I've seen the same specialists back home. A thick cloud of guilt seeps under the door and enters my room. I ask myself: If I'm Christian, if I believe in eternal life, why do I fight so hard to find answers? Why can't I accept that there may not be a solution to my problem?

I decide that I've had enough. I call my wife and tell her I'm coming home.

As I talk to her, I glance out the window and watch people come and go from the Mayo as the sun casts its final shadow over the City. I sit in my hotel room and study the darkness slowly consuming Rochester. I fixate on the marble exterior of the Clinic. I focus my attention on the statue of the universal man suspended naked above the sidewalk. Hanging up the phone, I leave the Kahler and return to the medical center.

"My wife called. She's going into labor," I say to the receptionist on the fifteenth floor of the Clinic, resorting to another lie. I watch impatiently as the woman begins re-scheduling the remainder of my visit for another day, another time. I walk away without agreeing to anything.

Exiting the Mayo Clinic, I no longer feel overwhelmed. Instead, I feel only freedom and settled satisfaction. Passing the naked man, I pause and examine the details of his emerald body.

I become quietly engaged by the sculptor's art as nightfall's modesty descends over the statue. Despite the onslaught of darkness, the naked man's arms remain open and upraised to heaven but I am unable to decide whether the man is yielding to, or arguing with, the Almighty.

A Fine Day

My father is getting on in years but time hasn't seemed to slow him down much. Oh, he's had the odd heart malady and the occasional back twinge resulting in surgery. These minor challenges seem to be appearing more regularly, evidence, despite his hardened demeanor, that age is creeping up on my old man. Still, as I watch him walk the far edge of the stubble, his Red Label Ruger twenty gauge held at port, his black Labrador retriever working the rippling stalks of dead corn, it's hard to believe Grandpa just turned seventy-five.

We're here, beneath a clear blue sky, on a gorgeous late October day, to celebrate our respective birthdays. North, across the flat table of land that we're hunting, a large pothole sits immobilized by early ice. There's a high ridge to the south, its spine covered in maple, aspen, and birch, the dead leaves of the slumbering trees chattering in the heavy breeze. Like everything around us, the leaves seem reluctant to let go. Summer has been long and dry. Autumn has been more of the same with folks golfing into October on the area courses, a circumstance usually unheard of north of Hinckley, Minnesota, the mythical line that divides north from south in this part of the State.

That we're hunting a game farm, a private plot of land in Northeastern Minnesota, intent upon shooting domesticated pheasants the owners of the place released earlier today doesn't reduce the serenity of the landscape or the impact of the occasion. The birds are skittish. They fly with quick abandon and native skill when flushed providing at least the appearance of a wild hunt.

My dad's dog stops dead in her tracks and goes on point. Sleek black fur reflects the morning sun. The Labrador's nose twitches and snuffles an insignificant dollop of broken corn.

"Watch her Mark," Dad yells.

"I'm on her," I reply.

The kid who is our guide for the day raises a twelve gauge automatic to his shoulder. I bring my twelve over-under to the ready. I take a step towards the dog.

Caaack. Caaack.

A beautiful rooster pheasant flushes from cover. Beating its wings to reach a meager altitude, the bird sets a course towards the pothole a few city blocks away.

Boom.

My first shot is low.

Boom.

My second shot is behind the fleeing rooster.

"I'm a little rusty," I admit as the three of us watch the pheasant sail across the frozen pond.

"That one's fox food," the guide muses.

As we continue our walk, I notice a pair of red tailed hawks soaring high above the open field.

"Hawks," I say, pointing up into the sky.

We stop to watch the raptors soar. The guide explains that the birds are here to collect pheasants that we miss, pheasants that foolishly set their sights on escaping into the forest with the misguided belief they can outwait danger. Most of the escaped birds will perish within a day, their ability to outwit predators dulled by generations of domestication.

Another pheasant flushes in front of me. I take my time, following the low course of the hen until it is out a safe distance before pulling the trigger of my shotgun.

Boom.

"Nice shot," my old man says as the dull gray bird folds and drops to the ground.

"Thanks."

Cleo retrieves the pheasant with style. The Labrador holds the bird firmly in her mouth as she trots through swaying grass and corn.

"Here girl," I urge.

The dog stops at my side and deposits the dead hen on frozen ground.

"Good girl," I praise, stroking the ebony fur of the dog's neck.

Cleo's long pink tongue slides in and out of her mouth. Droplets of spit fly into the cold air as she pants. The morning is just beginning. There is much work left to be done. There's little patience in the dog for sitting around when she knows there are birds to be hunted. She impatiently moves into a virgin section of corn, clearly indicating to her companions that break time is over.

Several pheasants take wing only to meet steel shot before I miss another bird, reminding me that I am, at the core, a mediocre marksman. My dad hits every bird he aims at. The age thing, I decide, is vastly overstated. We work the marsh surrounding the pond. I draw the job of stomping through the rushes and cattails with the dog. I learn that the ice doesn't support my weight. My boots break through. My feet get wet. There's nothing to do but trudge on.

Caaack.

A brilliantly hued rooster explodes from a tangle of alders, acting more like a ruffed grouse than a pheasant as it takes wing.

Boom.

The bird glides on.

Boom.

The rooster achieves the far side of the pond with impunity.

"Damn," I curse, opening the breech of my shotgun. Two spent shells drop into my gloved hand.

"You get him?" Dad asks from behind a veil of brush.

"Nope. He's hawk food," I reply, sliding two new shells into the gun's chamber.

A few steps later, I miss a hen that was keeping the escaped rooster company. The bird seems to stagger momentarily at the report of my second shot but I remain unconvinced that any pellets hit home. My dad and the guide take Cleo to work the edge of a logging road that marks the limit of the swamp. The hen I missed landed somewhere near the road. After a concerted effort, the bird flushes. My dad's desperate shot falls short. Another pheasant escapes.

"Missed her," my old man admits with regret.

I study my dad. He stands next to his dog on top of a slight rise, his orange hunting hat and vest stark and vibrant against the autumn sun. In middle age, he would have been angry at missing a bird. Now, deep into maturity, there is a calm acceptance about him that seems foreign in a man who has always lived life at seventy-eight rpm. It doesn't seem to bother him that a bird has flown free. It's just not that important.

I take Cleo down an old logging road near where one of the escaping roosters landed. The ridge marking the southern boundary of the old farm rises off my left shoulder, its pitch steep and covered with hardwoods. I work a thicket of wild raspberries with the dog. Nothing. I work a patch of young aspen. Nothing. The Labrador is spent. Her tail has ceased wagging. She's ready for a well-earned nap in the back seat of my dad's Chevrolet Tahoe.

As I round a bend in the trail, a fat male pheasant saunters into the open. The bird hesitates in the middle of the path. Cleo is so tired she doesn't even know the rooster has broken from cover. I stop. The dog continues to work the edge of the path. The bird twitches and then explodes into the yellow sky. Cleo breaks into a trot. I wait until the rooster is well above the dog.

Boom.

The bird flits away from the first shot and turns to take advantage of a strong gale blowing in from the east.

Boom.

The last pheasant of the day falls to earth.

Too Fat Horse

Dylan, my second son was twelve years old when my wife's beloved quarter horse mare, Cisco, died. Cisco was the best horse we ever owned. Anyone could ride her, from the most experienced horseman to the smallest child. When the mare passed away, it fell upon me to find her replacement.

"Here's an interesting horse," I told my wife René one night after supper as I perused the want ads. "A POA, ready to foal, for $1,200.00."

My wife, never all that enamored with horses, simply nodded her head.

"You don't even know what a POA is, do you?" I challenged.

"No, but I'm sure I'm about to find out."

"It stands for 'Pony of America'. Sort of the Dodge Dakota of horses, midsized between a horse and a pony."

"And we need this animal for what reason?" my spouse asked.

I looked at René over the edge of the newspaper.

"Dylan needs a horse."

"I'm not so sure Dylan is all that keen on owning a horse," my wife added as she put the last of the dinner dishes away.

Dylan seemed interested, interested enough to drive with me to a farm outside Cloquet to look at the pony. When we arrived at the place, a ramshackle outfit wedged in between stands of greening maples, with the last of winter's snow slowly melting off the pasture, I recognized the folks who owned the farm.

"How's it going, Doug?" I asked.

"You're the one who called about the horse?" the guy asked, shaking my hand. He wasn't a good friend. He had dated a friend of a friend. You know, one of those deals.

"Yep. This is my son, Dylan. The horse is for him. He's just beginning to ride."

A mild breeze rearranged my son's thick blond hair as he studied the farmer through a sideways glance. Dylan rarely looks someone head on, preferring to mosey up to the person before letting his piercing blue eyes lock in on the target.

"Pleased to meet you," the man said, offering my son his hand.

The kid responded with a half-hearted handshake.

"We're working on the handshake thing," I advised through a less-than-loving grimace.

"My daughter Tiffany is selling the horse. She's had the mare for a couple of years. The stud's that big stallion over there," the farmer said, indicating a massive black creature standing tethered to a cedar rail fence. "I was just about to mate him with one of my paint mares. Does Dylan want an education in the birds and the bees?"

I'm not sure that my son wanted to see the procreative process of making a foal. But I sure did. I'll spare you the details. Suffice it to say, the stallion was impressive.

After the breeding lesson, Tiffany brought us into the barn where the POA was patiently waiting. As we walked into the subtle light of the old dairy building, one thought struck me when I saw Starlight, the POA.

That is one fat horse, I said to myself.

There was little question in my mind that the animal was pregnant. Her belly was enormous.

A girl jumped from the top of the stall wall onto the horse's back and rode the animal around the pen. The mare trotted gently, never evincing any bad propensities.

"How long until she foals?" I asked.

"Should be a month or so," Tiffany advised.

"Can she be ridden until then?"

"I wouldn't advise it," the girl stated plainly. "She's gained a lot of weight. I'd take it easy on her," the teenager added.

A deal was struck standing in the dim light of a late April day amidst the landscape of rural Carlton County. A few days later, Star joined my quarter horse gelding Harry in our pasture. The POA seemed to fit right in.

Not knowing what to expect from a pregnant horse, I called our veterinarian, Dr. Meagher, to look at the horse. The vet came out, drew some blood to check for diseases, and gave the mare the once-over. She didn't do a formal pregnancy test on Star because the animal was obviously with foal.

"That is one fat horse," our friend Nancy McVean commented sometime later when René was showing off our latest equine purchase.

"She's pregnant," my wife advised.

"How neat for the kids," Nancy offered.

"They've seen Labrador puppies and several litters of kittens being born," René added. "But this should be something special."

Another month went by. Starlight continued to gain weight. I managed to get close enough to her motherly parts to determine that nothing seemed to be happening.

"Can you get Dr. Meagher to come out and preg test the horse?" I asked René one day over the telephone while I was at work. "She's getting bigger but I don't see any signs that she' ready to give birth".

"Sure."

I wasn't there for the pelvic examination conducted by my wife and Dr. Meagher. But, as reported to me by reliable sources, it consisted of my wife holding the mare's snout in a binder to prevent her from kicking the good doctor as the Vet stuck her entire right arm, all the way to the shoulder, up inside the animal, after which Dr. Meagher declared:

"This horse isn't pregnant. She's just fat."

I'll spare you the protracted machinations that transpired once I found out that the sellers had only owned the horse for a few months before they sold her to us. It turned out the "with foal" part of the advertisement was stretching the truth, so to speak. What's important is not what I did upon discovering the horse's true condition but what our kind friends Nancy McVean and Kathy Kaneski did afterwards.

Sometime later that summer, Mrs. Kaneski and Mrs. McVean took it upon themselves to conduct an investigation of the pharmacy department of our local Target store.

"Mark, Kathy and I have a present for you," Nancy announced a few days after she and Kathy visited Target.

The announcement came as Kathy, Nancy, and I sat around a picnic table at the McVean place on Island Lake. René was wading in the Lake as the two women and I sipped ice tea.

I know from past experience that both ladies are excellent cooks. My mouth began to salivate at the thought of homemade apple pie or brownies. Heck, Kathy, if I remember right, owed me a birthday dinner at the time. *Maybe there's a nice rib eye steak sizzling on the grill at the Kaneski place, right next door to the McVean's*, I theorized, *in satisfaction of that debt.*

"René, you have to see this too," Nancy urged, calling my wife away from the water.

Kathy produced a large white box wrapped smartly with gift foil and ribbon from beneath the table.

"Here," the women said in unison, "we hope this helps."

Their comment caused a puzzled look to form on my face.

Help? I thought to myself. *Help what?*

"Open it," Kathy urged.

I undid the ribbon and tore through the wrapping paper. I was greeted with a large hand-written label, the initials "HPT" prominently stenciled across the paper.

"HPT?" I asked.

"Horsie Pregnancy Test," Nancy advised.

Inside the box was a contraption of careful design pieced together from various kitchen utensils. It was obvious from the extensive hand written instruction pamphlet and the device's complex engineering that Mrs. McVean and Mrs. Kaneski had spent the better part of a Saturday creating the implement after carefully inspecting each and every brand of human EPT kit in the Target pharmacy. The women, including my wife, erupted in laughter. There was no question they were not laughing with me. They were laughing at me. I never cracked a smile.

"The next time you think the mare is pregnant," Nancy advised through a significant smile, "pull out the old HPT."

"You expect me to put this thing..." I began to ask.

"Precisely," Mrs. Kaneski said. "Just make sure the horse pees directly on the Popsicle stick."

Gone to the Dogs

Despite all the columns I've written for the *Star* over the past six or so years, I don't think I've devoted more than a couple of my essays to dogs. And since dogs and country life go together like teenagers' bedrooms and moldy socks, I think it's about time I addressed the current status of canines at the Munger place.

First, a little history.

My wife René and I tried the dog thing in town. I surprised our eldest son Matthew on his fourth Christmas by bringing home the cutest brown and black Beagle pup you've ever seen. I knocked on the door and then hid off to the side. The pup sat in a box on our front porch, a note from Santa fastened to a ribbon around the dog's neck.

"Matthew," René called out, "there's a package for you."

The toddler scooted across the thick living room carpet and bolted out the front door. It was instant love. And instant disaster.

Turns out that Beagles have some really nasty habits. I've always been a big dog person. I grew up with Labradors and Golden Retrievers. My wife is from a "non-dog" family. We really didn't know anything about small canines. It soon became apparent that the Beagle, who wore the moniker "Corky", was hell on paws.

First it was the furniture. Our living room couch was shredded. Then the puppy destroyed a freshly painted basement floor with his sharp claws. I tried to practice patience. Even when Doc Roach, our neighbor and the UMD Tennis Coach, tromped through our backyard to lodge a protest on behalf of the entire neighborhood about Corky's incessant howling, I still held out hope that the dog would change.

It wasn't like he was evil. Corky was loving. But when he was left alone, things happened. Bad things. After urinating on the already tattered aforementioned couch and being tossed outside, the dog got the bright idea to challenge rush hour traffic on St. Marie Street. He ended up with a broken leg. Ever seen a Beagle in a little white cast? Pathetic.

Once the cast was off, things didn't get any better. A ski trip to Lutsen with friends ended early when the dog threw up on the white cloth interior of our Honda Prelude. The nurses that responded to our want ad proclaiming "Free to a Good Home" were duly warned. We never heard back from them. I assume they had better luck training the Beagle than we did.

We were dogless when we moved to the country. There was an old doghouse behind the Sears home we purchased on the Cloquet River. The doghouse became home to Pelly, my brother David's aging Golden Retriever. Dave was in college. He lived in Duluth. His landlord prohibited dogs. Dave managed to keep Pelly with him through the better part of a school year until he was found out. That's when the retriever came to live with us.

There are lots of things I could say about Pelly. He was a true character. A shaggy mop of yellow fur and four legs that could out drink a men's softball team. All one had to do was flip over a Frisbee, fill it with beer, and the dog was life of the party, wagging his tail to tunes by Queen, Uriah Heap, and other Seventies bands. He ended up with the nickname "Pelkie the Finnish Wonder Dog" because he tolerated a hot sauna, despite his thick mane, better than most humans. And, through it all, he was a heck of a hunting dog (See *The Long Retrieve* at p.56 of **River Stories**).

After Pelly died, my family owned a succession of other dogs, which brings me to the recent past.

In 1999, we began building a new home. At the time, we owned two dogs and three horses. We sold the horses. But dogs, well, they're family. We had a serious problem. The apartment we rented in Hermantown while our house was being constructed wasn't a place for large dogs. And our two Labradors, Maggie, a black, and Sam, a yellow, are indeed large. Luckily, the new owners of our old home suggested that

67

we leave the dogs with them. Barb and Jim Kaas, the new owners, brought a Noah's Ark of critters to our old farmstead; assorted horses along with cats and dogs of various descriptions. We left the Labs behind in Fredenberg with the Kaas family during our six-month stay in the City of Quality Living.

When we moved back to Fredenberg Township, Maggie and Sam rejoined us. Temporarily. You know that adage about teaching old dogs new tricks? Well, both of our Labs are getting on in years. They seemed to enjoy their brief stay at the new house but eventually wandered back to the old place. Despite efforts to curb their behavior, they deserted us. I held out little hope that the Labs would return. I suspected the food must be a lot better Up River.

Sometime later, Sam, nearing thirteen years of age, ventured back to the new house. No new attractions were added at our place; no changes in the dog food supply occurred to entice his return. Maybe be grew tired of the hubbub across the pasture. Maybe he needed a secluded place to contemplate the universe. He's been in failing health for the past two years and maybe he realized that his time is drawing to a close. Or perhaps he simply wanted to be with his family.

Not long after Sam's return, I received a telephone call at work.

"Dad", my eldest son Matt said, "I need a favor."

"What's that?" I asked, feeling my wallet begin to lighten.

"One of the residents I work with was given a puppy. He can't have pets. I said I'd take her home and find a place for her."

I considered the information.

"I'm not so sure that's a good idea," I replied.

"Dad, it's only for a while," my son begged.

I softened.

"OK, but only until Friday. If she's not gone by then, I'll take her to the animal shelter myself."

"Thanks."

When Matt bought a leash for the dog and a matching collar with the name "Daisy May" etched on a copper nametag, further discussion of the matter became pointless.

I have to admit that Daisy's a cute runt. Black, short, and thin, with houndy ears. I have no idea of her lineage. But she's well-mannered, house broken, and, as you've likely suspected, already integrated into the family.

Again, this story is far from complete. The presence of a young pup at the house apparently awakened Maggie's maternal urges. A month later, our obese female black Lab waddled down the road, sauntered up the main staircase, and perched herself under the covered front porch of the new house.

We were once dogless. An aging patriarch returned to his family. A young upstart arrived to keep the old dog company. And then, the queen of the feed bin returned.

Only in the country.

René's Fence

"The darn deer are at it again," my wife lamented.

She was standing ankle deep in the sandy loam of her vegetable garden surveying broken corn stalks and nibbled bean shoots.

"We need a fence."

I'd approached the garden to talk to her about transplanting four apple trees we'd brazenly placed along the edge of our pasture surrounding our new house. My belief that the trees would be safe from attack by hungry white tailed deer was misguided. Within weeks of being set in the firm dry ground the new trees had been reduced to stalks of slender trunk, denuded and devoid of leaves and branches. It was obvious that any fruit trees we wanted to plant would require greater security from our cloven hoofed neighbors.

"I'm gonna move the apple trees to alongside your garden," I responded. "Then when I build a fence, they'll be protected from the deer."

"You sure the trees are worth saving?"

I already knew the chance of the stubs reclaiming their vitality was slim. I didn't let reality dissuade me.

"I think they'll be all right if we can keep the critters at bay," I added.

At our old house, a mere 200 yards upstream, our vegetable garden, flower gardens, and fruit trees had never experienced damage from deer. Whether because of the electric fence surrounding our horse pasture or because of the close proximity of our two Labradors, the deer stayed away. It was a shock to learn how clever and insistent white tails can be once we moved onto the new place. It didn't help that our dogs chose to remain behind at our old Sears house once we moved. But that, as they say, is another story.

I'm not the most proficient carpenter. However, I can, with some guidance, build a respectable fence. René took advantage of my meager skills. A few days after our conversation, she deposited t-posts and wire livestock fencing on the ground next to the freshly tilled soil of the vegetable garden. I think she envisioned that the fence would erect itself within a matter of minutes.

A July sun hung morbidly over our field. Wet air enveloped me as I began the process of clawing at the parched soil with a post-hole digger. I intended to use reclaimed cedar posts for the corner supports of my fence because erecting t-posts alone wouldn't allow me to pull the wire mesh snug. I glanced at the deer-ravaged vegetables as sweat rolled off me like water pours from a pitcher and wondered whether the effort was worth it.

"The fence is looking good," René interjected at various intervals during the project. "But don't you think that post over there is a little out of line?"

Her veiled criticism flew across my sunburned brow like a cannon shot across the bow of Old Ironsides.

"You want it straighter? How about picking up the sledge hammer and lending a hand?" I retorted, muttering additional comments beneath my breath.

"You're doing such a nice job," my wife demurred, ignoring my jab. "I'd hate to have one or two posts detract from the finished product."

René's proffered compliment did not mollify me.

"I thought you'd be further along by now," she added with just the right hint of sarcasm, as she turned towards the house.

I'd started the project early Sunday morning, missing church, violating the commandment about working on the Sabbath into the bargain. I sinfully labored straight through the noon hour, pausing only in the late afternoon to cool my scarlet skin in the slow current of the Cloquet River. I also took to the water to avoid further conversations with René. She had expected that the fence would be completed in a day. The project was still a long way from fruition. Rather than engage in doomed dialogue, I chose to cool off.

The River. We're facing a major drought, at least in terms of flowage out of Island Lake, the large man-made reservoir formed by the Cloquet River a mile and a half upstream from

71

our place. Despite the deluge of rain we were blessed with during late spring and early summer, the level of the watercourse passing our home is at an all time low. Wading in the River, cold water from the very bottom of Island Lake numbing my legs and hips, I longed for depth. I made do with a headlong plunge into waist-deep water to rid my body of the sun's intensity.

Dog-tired, I slept soundly that night, rising on Monday morning to the rigidity and stubborn pain of a middle-aged body. Monday evening after work I pieced together the final sections of fencing.

"Where do you want the gate?"

"By the compost pile," René responded.

I began to tear into nearly dead sod, the grass brittle from the lack of rain, with the claws of the post-hole digger. A half-hour later, admiring my proficiency, ready to run the last of the fencing, I realized we'd made a mistake.

"I think the gate should be over by the garden shed," I offered, pointing in the direction of a gleaming white building on the north side of the garden patch. "It makes more sense over there."

I stared hard at the cedar posts I'd just erected with the realization that my most recent effort had been a waste of time.

"I think you're right," René agreed.

"The gate will have to wait until tomorrow. I need to pick up some treated lumber and hinges."

A brief flash of disappointment clouded my wife's features.

"Will it be done tomorrow?"

"Yes," I responded, choosing my words carefully so as to avoid a lengthy discussion.

The truth was that I'd been forced to redo many of the t-posts along the way as the path of the fence drifted out of line. I didn't want to stand around justifying the time I'd expended. I just wanted the work done.

"Like my gate?" I said, beaming proudly as my wife approached the finished enclosure on Tuesday evening. I'd spent the better part of another three hours manufacturing the gate for René's garden fence.

René opened the stainless steel latch and pulled the door towards her.

"It needs to be higher off the ground."

Blood began to surge into my neck.

"Fine," I responded, proceeding to unscrew the chrome hinges.

Another hour passed. The deer flies and horse flies that had plagued me over three days diminished, replaced by nearly invisible mosquitoes. Between angry swats at insects, I managed to re-hang the gate, trimming the jam so that the door swung freely and fit snugly against its frame.

"That's better," René said after her final appraisal of the project was complete. "You know, the deer have stayed away since you began building the fence," she added in an attempt at conversation.

I didn't respond. My legs carried me to our back porch where an old pair of cutoff jeans hung wet and heavy over the railing. Under the cover of a beach towel, I undressed and slid the shorts over my feet before lumbering with age towards the waiting River. Immersed in the flow, I watched dusk overtake the heat of the day. Details of the shoreline disappeared. The intricacies of the forest vanished. Individual trees merged and formed a singular black silhouette against a velvet blue evening sky.

"I wonder where the deer are?" I asked quietly as I looked across the parched grass and admired my handiwork.

Another Deer Story

Those of you who know me know that I am not much of a hunter and even less of a deer hunter. The last time I seriously stalked whitetail I did so on the spur of the moment with a borrowed shotgun loaded with slugs and wound up haggling with another hunter over the six point buck that I'd knocked down. That incident pretty much soured me on the whole business of going into woods of Northeastern Minnesota during deer season.

This year, with an over-abundance of deer around our country home, I decided to buy a hunting license. My plan was to hunt the woods some distance away from our house while remaining on our land. In anticipation of the hunting opener in November, I took to the woods while the leaves were still in color to build deer stands out of salvaged lumber and aspen logs. Things were set for a good hunt.

The Opener. I climbed into one of my new stands before sunrise. I was already comfortable when Gunner Johnson (that's a real Minnesota name now isn't it?) and another guy I'd given permission to hunt my land, ambled by. I whistled. The pair of sleepy hunters kept right on walking.

The forest was quiet. There was significant sun. It was warm, not at all reminiscent of the deer hunting weather of my youth. What I remember from nearly every hunt with my father and younger brother at our old shack up by Comstock Lake was shivering; from the moment I sat down in my stand to the moment I walked back to the shack at the end of the day. It didn't matter whether I walked, sat in a stand, or found an outlook on a ridge near a swamp. I was always chilled, cold to the very bone. Not this year.

Sometime after eight in the morning I heard the snap of a branch. I'd already been fooled by innumerable red squirrels darting across leaves decaying on the ground. The noise disturbed the gentle slumber I'd fallen into. I forced my eyes open, sat heavily in my stand, and wondered whether another rodent was toying with me.

74

Then I saw her. Her movements were as muted as conditions would allow. The doe stopped moving and stared at me but the sound of ground debris being crushed didn't cease. There was another deer following the doe. I had no doe permit and don't really believe in shooting does, though now with the deer population so high, I'm beginning to think we need to take more females to insure that the herd is controlled and doesn't succumb to disease or starvation. In any event, the doe studied my location. I waited for its companion to show itself.

The second animal hesitated, its neck and head concealed by a conifer, as it walked slowly behind the doe. A slight wind came up and pushed my scent towards the deer. Before I could react, the flags of the two animals went up, and they were gone.

Despite the warmth of the sun, my toes began to get cold. I decided to take a walk. Unloading my twelve gauge over-under of its slugs, I climbed out of the stand and set out towards the Taft Road. My plan was to follow the road for a few hundred yards and then turn into the woods and meander through a cedar swamp along the banks of a small creek that feeds the Cloquet River on the eastern-most border of our land.

I climbed a small rise next to the road, loaded my shotgun, and entered the forest. As I reached the shadow of the trees, two deer bolted. The animals leaped over a fallen aspen, their brown and white bodies graceful against the sunshine, before vanishing in the cedar swamp. Even if I had a doe permit, I wouldn't have taken a shot. I couldn't. I was frozen by the simple grace of the animals.

I hunted hard the remainder of the day. After lunch, Christian, my third son, joined me. He sat quietly alongside me in another stand. After an unproductive hour or so, I left my son and took a short walk in an attempt to drive deer. I pushed a doe past Chris but saw no bucks. As the sun set, my son and I met up and began our short walk home.

Strolling down our driveway, the sky turning to faint orange as it disappeared in the west, does and fawns appeared as silhouettes across the brown grass of the pasture surrounding our house. My son and I looked at each other and

75

smiled, thankful that the bucks remained concealed saving us from further humiliation.

The next evening. Nightfall wrapped my wife's Toyota RAV tightly as I drove the vehicle. Like an enormous ghost, a buck manifested in the middle of the gravel lane leading to our house.

"Holy moly," I muttered.

"He's gotta go eight points," René whispered.

"Ten," Chris corrected from the back seat of the SUV.

The buck was ancient and obviously far smarter than the dozens of men and women hunting the woods surrounding our property. The animal took a deep breath. Steam curled off the buck's fur. The vapor framed the animal's magnificent rack before he turned and fled into the safety of the marsh.

We drove further. As the Toyota rounded a corner and climbed towards our garage, two shadows blocked our path.

"I can't believe it," I muttered.

"Not again," Chris moaned.

There in our driveway stood another trophy buck, an eight pointer, and his female companion.

I guess there isn't much more to say about that, now is there?

A Little White Lie

"What happened to your finger?" I asked my son Dylan, who was, at the time, thirteen years old.

"I jammed it playing shinny hockey in Nick's basement," Dylan replied matter-of-factly, never hesitating, never missing a beat.

I stared hard at the index finger of my boy's left hand. The second knuckle was swollen red.

"You sure you don't want to have it looked at?" I offered.

"Nah, it's OK."

Fast forward to a funeral about a week later. Heavy pipe organ music echoes from the thick stone walls of St. Paul's Episcopal Church in Duluth. Mourners gather to pay their final respects to the wife of one of my former law partners. It's a contemplative moment. The weight of mortality hangs heavy on those assembling in the church pews.

"Hi Tracey," I say to Nick's mom. She's sitting behind me. We're both waiting for the sobering litany of the funeral mass to begin. "Dylan's finger is still pretty swollen from that floor hockey game in your basement."

"Oh," the woman responds through a smile.

We move on and discuss how it is that each of us knew the deceased. The music flares. The service begins. My eyes divert to reflect upon the thick wood beams and high ceiling of the cathedral. Ever the perfectionist, I note that, despite expensive repairs to the building's roof, water stains remain visible against the stark white plaster of the sanctuary.

I'm cognizant that Dylan is visiting his doctor today, and is in fact, likely at the physician's office that very moment. Dr. Knutsen will examine my son and doubtlessly x-ray the knuckle of the left index finger to insure no bones have been broken, no ligaments torn, as an aftermath of the floor hockey incident. René has taken off work to be there with our son. Things will go smoothly.

Tracey taps me on my shoulder. I turn to face her. Her eyes are clear and somewhat hesitant. She speaks in a quiet, kind tone of voice.

"Mark, about Dylan's finger..."

"Yes?"

"Well, I don't really want to tattle on him but, that's not how he got hurt."

"What?"

There's a short gap in our dialogue. Sacred music fills the background with reverent tones.

"He and Jake were shooting at each other with BB guns. I think there's a BB stuck in Dylan's finger."

A vision of my wife sitting in Dr. Knutsen's office, having related my son's version of events to the physician, becoming overwrought as the terrible truth is suddenly and certainly revealed to her by x-ray, saunters into my mind.

"Are you sure?"

"Positive," the woman whispers. "I feel awful having to tell you this."

"Don't. I appreciate it."

There is no way that I can diplomatically leave. Instead, I whisper a prayer on my wife's behalf that the service will end soon enough for me to reach her by telephone. I inject my selfish plea along with those directed by the congregation on behalf of the departed.

"This is Mark Munger," I say urgently, talking to a nurse on the telephone after the service has ended. "I need to talk to René before Dr. Knutsen sees Dylan."

"You're too late, Mr. Munger. The x-rays have already been taken. The doctor is in the examination room with your wife and son."

As René later related the incident, the physician walked into the exam room, our son's finger swollen and throbbing with severe pain, placed the developed film on the view box, and left mother and child alone to consider the image before them.

"What do you suppose that is?" René remarked, pointing to a shadow on the film, clueless as to what was actually wrong with Dylan's finger.

"Maybe it's one of those marker things that they use," Dylan suggested.

"Maybe."

Dr. Knutsen wandered back into the room. He held his face tight with his right hand to suppress a smile. His other hand held a laser pointer. With the click of a switch, a red dot appeared on the surface of the x-ray. The pointer came to rest on the circular artifact displayed on the film.

"What do you suppose this might be?" the doctor asked our second son.

René became uneasy at the tone of the inquiry. She shifted anxiously in her chair. Her eyes scrutinized Dylan's face. Something was up. She wasn't certain what was going on. But something was up.

The boy remained silent.

"I don't think it came from playing floor hockey, do you?"

More silence from the patient.

"Dylan?"

"I guess not," the teenager finally admitted.

"What do you think it might be?" the doctor repeated.

"It could be a BB, I guess," the lad offered as his mother's mouth dropped open in utter surprise.

Of course, I wasn't there for this part of the story. I was standing in the social hall of St. Paul's Episcopal Church trying to envision what was occurring in the doctor's office. What I imagined wasn't far from the truth.

Turtles

I have the opinion, based upon personal experience, that turtles are archaic animals that simply do not understand automobiles.

Every year that we've lived in the country, ancient snapping turtles, their protective dark green shells covered with prehistoric nodules, their beaks wicked and curved, have sought out loose sand and gravel on our property in which to deposit their eggs.

When we lived at the old place, before building our present house, I annually encountered huge female snappers digging up our vegetable garden to secure their clutches of eggs. In fact, there's an old photograph of me standing proudly on the newly mown grass of our front lawn at the old house. I'm holding a snapper at arm's length by its tail. It's clear from the picture that the heavy weight of the animal is straining my arm as the turtle hangs precariously in the thick summer air. I caught that turtle as she planted her eggs in the moist soil of our potato mounds. The photograph was taken just before I released the animal back into the Cloquet River that runs through our property.

Sometimes I skinny-dip in the River. It's not infrequent that I speculate that the same mother turtle, or one of her descendents, lurks in the dark water beneath the River's overhanging bank, waiting to lash out at something resembling a …Well, you get the picture. As a male, it isn't a happy thought.

Though such an assault has never materialized, once, a few years ago on nearby Island Lake, a big snapper did bite my niece Kelly's big toe as she dangled it over the side of an inflatable Fun Island on a hot Fourth of July afternoon. I view that attack as verification that my manly nightmare is likely a vision shared by a dim-witted turtle or two.

Our new house has a quarter mile long gravel driveway that passes over the throaty gurgle of an unnamed creek. The road pre-existed the new house. For years my wife and I have walked the gravel road to access a system of hiking trails cutting through our land. Virtually every summer, we find a snapping turtle hunkered down in the middle of the gravel road laying her eggs.

Driving home from work last week, as I approached the area where the little creek passes beneath the road, I came upon not one, not two, but three semi-buried snapping turtles depositing their offspring-to-be in the warm gravel of the road.

"Jack, look at the momma turtles," I exclaimed, stopping my van just short of the preoccupied reptiles.

My three and a half year old son sat upright in his car seat. I rolled down the window on his side of the mini van so that he could see the snappers more clearly.

"Turtles," he cooed.

"They're laying eggs."

The drawback to having turtles use our driveway as a nursery was reinforced the next day. When I returned from work Wednesday evening with Jack and his sixteen year old brother Dylan in my Lumina van, one of the smaller turtles remained lodged in her hole. I exited the van. Dylan soon followed. I pushed an alder branch in front of the animal's mouth. The turtle blinked but did not snap her jaws at the stick.

"Something drove over it," Dylan remarked. "There's a crack in its shell."

My son pointed to a thin line crossing the turtle's military green covering. There was no question a vehicle had driven over the animal disrupting the protective bone.

"Must have been the garbage man," I replied, grasping the tail of the injured animal.

The turtle did not move. It was obvious that the weight of the refuse truck had crushed the reptile's spine. The animal was alive but paralyzed. Clear water swirled below the edge of the roadway as I hoisted the snapper and launched her towards the creek.

Splash.

The turtle landed heavily in the shallows. The snapper's head rose above the broiling water. It was apparent that the animal could not resist the force of the stream as her body spun in the watercourse.

"Something will come along and eat her," I reflected, getting back into my vehicle.

A day or two later, Jack and I were driving the narrow causeway between the Eagle's Nest and Blue Max Resorts where the Beaver River spreads out to form Fish Lake. A bright sun and no clouds soared high above the shimmering shoreline. There on the hot blacktop, a painted turtle, significantly smaller and less ominous than its fearsome snapping cousins, stood poised to cross against traffic. I stopped the car.

"Stay in your seat," I admonished Jack.

The turtle made no attempt to evade me as I approached it.

When my hands closed around its smooth shell, the animal defensively retracted its head, tail, and limbs.

"See what daddy found?" I asked my son as I held the mud turtle towards my son inside the van. Before Jack answered, the tortoise released a deluge of clear liquid onto the carpeting.

"Turtle," Jack cooed.

"A mud turtle," I responded. "Not a snapper but it can still bite."

Later that evening, my son Chris and his youngest brother released the painter in the pond of our rock garden. The artificial limits of René's garden pool did not deter the animal. Within a matter of minutes, the turtle was determinedly digging in the sandy loam of our front yard. When she was done, a dozen or so small eggs filled the hole that she'd created to ensure another generation of painted turtles.

Confronting the Green Eyed Monster

I was reading the Sunday *Duluth News Tribune*. My reading pattern is constant. It's always the sports, the comics (my eyes grow fuzzy trying to find the hidden picture in that one strip), the arts section, and then the news. I stick to this order regardless of what may have happened in the world. There is something comforting in consistency.

The arts section is a new interest, one spurred on by my recently acquired propensity for writing. As a white middle-aged, middle-class male, I am profoundly competitive. I read the arts blurbs to discover what other writers, artists, and poets are up to in the Northland: what new pieces they've written, what awards they've been blessed with. I have a fierce inner angst for vindication, a desire to feel that my efforts at writing and self-publishing have some greater meaning. Reading about others who are walking the same path, fighting the same battle, generally does that for me.

This Sunday, I read with great interest a piece in the *News Tribune* about a Proctor woman who, after moving to the Twin Cities, wrote her first novel in her late thirties. Since I also began to write in earnest later in life, my initial reaction to the article was:

"How neat- another writer who started late is getting her due."

Her name is Sarah Stonich. The book is **These Granite Islands.** Like my debut novel, **The Legacy**, Ms. Stonich's book is set on the Iron Range of Minnesota. Unlike my book, a large New York Publishing House picked hers up. My book is published by Savage Press of Superior, Wisconsin, a small, one man effort captained by Mike Savage. The difference between being published by Little Brown and Savage Press cannot be overstated.

Along with the national marketing power of a large publishing house, authors lucky enough to find a mainstream publisher also sign lucrative contracts which pay a generous cash advance. Like any major player in the game, Little Brown will also send Ms. Stonich across the country in promotion of her novel. She'll do reading and signing events at flagship bookstores in New York, Chicago and on the West Coast at the publisher's behest. I, on the other hand, continue to schedule my own events with minimal assistance from my publisher. It's not that Mike doesn't try; he does. But being a small publishing house means his efforts are concentrated on publishing first, marketing second.

When I discovered the measure of Ms. Stonich's success, I was unprepared for the extent of the envy that welled up inside me. Confronting a little bit of jealousy can be a helpful thing, spurring one to seek greater rhetorical mountains to climb. However, I was wholly unprepared for the rush of envy that overcame me as I read the *News Tribune*.

"This really irritates me," I confessed to my wife, the professional therapist in our home.

"What's that?"

"Oh, this woman from St. Paul. She writes some book about an old woman on the Iron Range and all of a sudden, she's an overnight sensation."

Of course, the underlying and unspoken sentiment was:

Why couldn't that be me? Why, after nearly seven months of constant personal marketing efforts on behalf of my little novel, why hadn't it won awards? Why didn't **The Legacy** *receive national acclaim?*

"Patience, Mark. It'll come."

"Yeah and you know how patient I am, René."

In truth, I'm one of the most impatient people I know. It's a trait that I struggle with at my "real" job, where, as a District Court Judge, I'm constantly called upon to exercise restraint. I'm nowhere done learning that facet of my job: I'm nowhere near being able to say, "I am a patient man."

I tossed the "Us" section of the *Tribune* aside. My wife's admonitions didn't curb the tacky, ugly feeling of resentment stuck in my craw. I knew better than to invoke God to deal with my sin. He or She has bigger fish to fry, so to speak, than to listen to me whining about my hobby.

I found my way into the three-season porch of our house on the banks of the Cloquet River. The room serves as my sanctuary, as my study. It's where I go to write, and sometimes, to read what others have written. Sitting heavily on a cushioned chair, mired in a cesspool of self-pity, I placed my feet on a stool and perused the latest issue of "Writer's Ask", a newsletter for neophyte authors published by *Glimmer Train* magazine.

Glimmer Train is one of the most beloved literary journals in the nation. I've entered short story after short story in the publication's writing contests. I've received rejection after rejection from the editors of the magazine: little notes of condolence that I file away with hundreds of other similar messages I've received from a variety of other publications. Despite the fact that *Glimmer Train* hasn't liked any of my stuff, I covet the writing displayed in the magazine. I consider it to be a guide, a "how to" manual of short story writing, which is the reason I subscribe to "Writer's Ask".

As I scanned various interviews with famous scribes contained in the newsletter, a curious thing occurred. Even though I'd followed my earlier inclination and refrained from asking the Almighty for intervention and guidance, a power beyond humanity interceded on my behalf. There, set out plainly on the printed page were words of sage advice from a world-renowned author:

Don't write for publication, write for yourself. Don't worry about what other writers are achieving; worry about your project and whether or not you are being true to yourself. Don't disregard envy but don't dwell upon it. Use small doses of jealousy to motivate you to work hard at your writing, at your craft.

The passage contained an answer. Maybe not <u>the</u> answer I was looking for, but clearly a thoughtful, well-reasoned response to dealing with the "green eyed monster" that was now lurked beneath my writing table. In reality, it was the same answer, stated in slightly different terms, as my wife's:

Be patient. Good things will come if you do the work. Keep your spirits up and remain true to yourself.

Sunday evening. I tried to get back to work on my second novel. My soul held too much residual envy for me to write productively. After creating several poorly constructed paragraphs, excerpts that will likely find the bottom of my wastebasket, I turned off my notebook computer and went outside to help my third son, Chris, put together a new trampoline. By nightfall, the three youngest Munger boys were leaping exuberantly through the cool evening air. Watching their antics, I felt the weight of my jealousy dissipate incrementally with each gleeful bounce.

When I got to work today, I turned on my computer, went online and visited Northern Lights Books, a local independent bookseller. I didn't need to peruse the store's selection of new offerings. I knew which book I wanted. Without hesitation, I bought **These Granite Islands.**

The Short Life of Doc the Bunny

"**I**'m buying Jack a bunny for Easter," my wife René advised over the cell phone as she drove towards Dan's Feed Bin in Superior, Wisconsin.

"I'm not so sure about the wisdom of that," I announced quietly.

"What? It's hard to hear you over the static."

I had already taken a risk by broaching the topic of early rodent death. I decided to keep my predictions to myself.

"It's not important," I shouted over the mouthpiece.

"What?"

I hung up the cell phone and concentrated on driving. I was on my way to pick up Jack at daycare. The rabbit would have to remain incognito for three days, until Easter Sunday when it could be revealed to our five year old son.

Easter. Things went well. The brown and white bunny hopped around the great room of our house depositing rabbit pellets in nearly every corner of the space. Jack chased him and cuddled him and learned about rabbit claws, ending up with scratches across both wrists that resulted in significant welts. I placed a cage in Jack's room on a child's table. Before leaving for church, I spread clean wood shavings in the bottom of the cage, freshened the rabbit's water, and added pellets to the food dish.

"What's the bunny's name?" I asked Jack as I drove to services.

"Doc," he replied without hesitation.

There was no sense asking how the kid came up with the name. He just had. I left it at that.

Christian, our third son, attempted to litter train Doc. He'd gone online and read up on the process. Apparently Doc was computer illiterate. He never really accepted the notion of pooping in a litter box. Instead, he chose any convenient corner of the room he was in to leave his mess. After a couple of weeks of little deposits of bunny pellets in the farthest reaches of the house, I put an end to the experiment. The litter box was relegated to the storage shed. The rabbit was confined to quarters.

Jack continued to love and cuddle Doc but wisely adopted the strategy of doing so only when wearing long sleeves. The scratches faded. The bunny grew.

"René," I said one day, looking at the box Doc's cage came in, "is Doc a dwarf rabbit?"

"No, he's a full sized rabbit."

"Well, there may be a problem. The cage you bought is for dwarf rabbits. Doc's still growing. He'll out-grow his cage."

"Do you always have to be so critical?"

After more than twenty years of marriage, I knew better than to respond. I walked out the back door, intent on providing Doc with outdoor grazing space. Shoots of new grass were appearing in the back yard. I'd promised my sister Annie that she could use our outdoor playpen, essentially a plastic corral that folds up for transport, for her little girl, Madeline. But the playpen seemed an ideal fence to house a new bunny. I found the contraption buried in tall weeds next to our storage shed and set it up. Immediately upon his release into the enclosure, the bunny began to munch.

Each morning before taking Jack to daycare I placed the rabbit in the enclosure. Jack would climb into the playpen, hold the growing bunny, stroke its smooth soft fur, and say a daily goodbye. I cautioned Christian and our eighteen year old son Dylan, to make sure our two Labradors remained in their kennels while the rabbit browsed. I'd seen enough Easter bunnies reduced to puffs of fur by our family dogs over the years to know that dogs don't understand the niceties involved in declaring a rodent to be a family pet.

Tuesday afternoon. I drove my Honda Passport SUV up the gravel drive towards the house after work. Jack chewed contentedly on a snack in the back seat. The sun was high. The day had been warm. I'd left the rabbit secure in its enclosure free to nibble clover to his heart's content. I parked the car in the garage and watched Jack exit the Honda and amble out the service door. A blood-curdling cry arose. I jumped out of my seat and raced to the door. Outside, I discovered that the bunny corral had been upended.

I rushed to Jack's side. Doc, or what had been part of Doc, rested between my son's tiny feet. Two blank eyes stared up at us from the rabbit's severed head. In the distance, Daisy, our mutt retriever, cowered in the deep grass, unwilling to make her presence obvious.

I carried Jack into the house, sat him down on the sofa, and bounded down the carpeted stairs leading to the lower level of our house.

"Who's the idiot who let Daisy out of her kennel?"

A lock clicked.

"Matt," Chris sheepishly revealed from behind the security of his locked door.

I stormed down the narrow hallway leading to my eldest son's bedroom.

"Matt," I yelled, throwing open the door to his room, "did you let Daisy out of her kennel?"

My eldest son works nights. My accusation rousted him from sleep.

"What?" he mumbled.

"Did you let your dog out of her kennel?" I repeated.

"Ya, so?"

"Well, she just tore the head off your brother's bunny," I seethed. "You walked right by the rabbit when you came home. How could you not put two and two together?"

"What?"

In danger of losing it, I withdrew.

"Jack," I said in as consoling a voice as I could muster when I rejoined my youngest son on the living room couch, "Doc is dead. Daisy didn't know any better. She's a dog. Dogs are supposed to chase rabbits. You stay here while I go outside, OK?"

Jack nodded. Tears streamed down his face.

Outside, I locked the offending canine back in her kennel, picked up the rabbit's head, walked to the edge of the trees, and gave the remains a heave. There was no sense in holding a funeral. It would only serve to upset Jack all over again.

By and by, Matt felt so bad about the whole ordeal that he and Chris drove Jack to the pet store in search of a replacement for Doc. I suggested something smaller, a Guiana pig or a hamster. Something that could remain inside, out of the reach of marauding dogs. Jack selected a white hamster with beady red eyes. He named her Shirley. The first time Jack picked Shirley up Shirley bit his pinky and drew blood. Then she learned how to escape from her cage by standing on her plastic igloo and squeezing through the bars.

One evening, Matthew knocked on the door to our bedroom. He'd been out with friends. The hamster had been AWOL for two days, her disappearance causing Jack mountains of little boy angst.

"Come in," René responded.

Our eldest son entered our bedroom. The bottom edge of his t-shirt was rolled up.

"I found the hamster," Matt said, holding the fabric of his shirt tightly to his stomach.

"Where?" René asked.

"She was running around in my room."

"Put her away," I mumbled, my head pressed against the softness of my pillow, "and go to bed."

"Goodnight," Matt said.

I listened as our eldest boy opened Shirley's cage. Immediately, the rodent found its metal wheel and began to run in place.

Squeak. Squeak. Squeak.

Likely getting in shape for another escape attempt, I thought as I faded off to sleep.

Last Chance

The sky is gray. The wind blows. Drips of rain slip down the trunks of the three birch trees supporting the deer stand I occupy. It's not my stand but one built by a friend. Ron Envall is a substantial guy. The platform reflects Ron's need to have a secure, sturdy place from which to scan the woods. The stand is constructed of treated 2"x 6" timbers, plywood, and twenty-penny spikes. The thing is built to hold Ron. It's excessively sturdy for a man of my size.

Everyone around me has been shooting deer. Does. Spike bucks. Mammoth swamp bucks with gargantuan racks. I've seen two deer. The flash of a tail and a snort of warning. The flank of a doe retreating through a swampy thicket. No chance for a shot. No need to discharge my over-under twelve gauge armed with slugs. Christian, my sixteen year old son, has had similar luck. He's heard a few animals crashing through the forest but has seen no deer.

Snow fell this past week. Snow dampens the sound of deer on the move and makes the animals less wary. Snow also provides contrast in the forest, making the deer easier to see. The snow has largely melted. What remains has been hardened by the early winter sun and polished smooth by recent rain. The deer are nervous. The noise of their hooves chattering over ice-covered trails has got them wary. The woods are crawling with humans. Deer hunters march endlessly through the forest in search of animals to shoot. The noise of the advancing florescent army forces the deer deep into the swamps. Given the circumstances, I'll be lucky to see any deer on this dismal day.

It's the last day of deer season. I've managed to get into the woods for a total of six hours of hunting. Book selling events in Canada and here at home in the States have eaten up prime hunting time. I missed opening day. Chris related that I really didn't miss much other than below zero cold. He fired no shots. He hit no deer. No venison was taken off our acreage.

91

I hunted the second day of the season. It warmed up enough to make the few hours I spent in Ron's stand enjoyable. There's something almost spiritual about sitting ten feet above the floor of the forest, a weapon in your hands, your ears and eyes tuned in to the sounds and sights of the woods, a slowly rising sun warming the bare skin of your face. But, as I've already confessed, I saw only glimpses of deer, phantoms that could not be shot during that earlier watch.

Today, the wind is brisk but does not chill. The drizzle is so light that it doesn't penetrate my clothing. I remove my fluorescent orange hat and gloves and sit silently amongst gently swaying trees. I place my shotgun across the corner supports of the stand and scan slight openings in the deep forest for signs of movement. I see nothing. Nothing but sedge grass, balsam, aspen, birch, and three large red pines, remnants of the forest that once covered this piece of land.

By the age of the pines, I speculate that the trees sprouted in the aftermath of the Great Cloquet Fire of 1918, a conflagration that consumed hundreds of thousands of acres of forest, destroyed entire cities and towns, and killed upwards of five hundred people. The red pines in front of me likely sprouted from soil blackened by that fire. The pines are impressive against the surrounding second-growth birch and aspen but are mere twigs in comparison to the white pine and red pine forest that once covered this part of Minnesota.

I hear rustling on the woodland floor. My ears perk up. I move my right hand towards the stock of the shotgun, alert and ready should a deer appear. A red squirrel skitters across ice. My heart returns to its normal pace.

Not long after the rodent disappears under the snow, I hear what sounds like a pair of bison crashing through the underbrush. There is no question that the noise is the result of a doe being chased by a buck in rut. The sound grows louder. The deer are moving closer. I slide my hands under my gun and lift the weapon to the ready. My index finger moves into position outside the trigger guard. The disturbance stops. I can tell from the direction of the noise that the deer are off to my right, concealed from view by a row of balsam. I try to control my breathing. The skin of my bare hands chills. I wait. And wait.

I never hear the deer again. Like ghosts in the mist, they vanish. I never see them, never have a chance of a shot. Dusk arrives. The rain intensifies. My glasses fog but I do not get wet. Distant gunfire booms from across the Cloquet River. I do not hear any shots fired on my side of the River.

Finally, it's too dark to hunt. I empty the breech of my shotgun and climb down Ron's well-built ladder until my hunting boots, the leather aged from use and lack of care, rest firmly on wet ground. I walk home. I have failed as a hunter. Still, I am satisfied.

A Bitter Harvest

After days of unrelenting cold and gray skies, the sun has finally decided to shine. It's Sunday afternoon. Dylan, my second son, is working at a local convenience store. Christian, my third son, is hiding somewhere on the lower level of our house with his buddy Spencer playing video games. Matt, the eldest Munger boy, is sitting in front of the television watching another putrid performance by the Minnesota Vikings. Jack, my youngest, is in his bedroom playing with action figures, his imagination aglow with possibilities.

The wind is raw despite the low globe of the sun hanging to the west. Dead cornstalks chatter in the breeze as I trudge through the wet loam of our vegetable garden. Narrow squash, colored bright orange and shaped like emaciated footballs, sit on moist ground. I hack at the vines with a hatchet, releasing the vegetables before dropping them gently into a waiting trailer attached to an old Yamaha four-wheeler. I haven't been in the garden for over a month. I despair at the weeds that have overtaken what was once a neat and orderly plot. Migrating raspberry canes choke out the blueberry bushes that René, my horticultural wife, planted last spring. A similar intrusion overshadows the new black raspberry canes that I planted with visions of sweet homemade jam in mind.

Huge acorn squash, the girth of their cylindrical shapes equal to a man's waist, the globes weighing in excess of thirty pounds, their skins still hard and green, prove to be a challenge as I hack them free of their vines and drop them over the fence onto our lawn. I stare at the squash. It seems impossible that these vegetables would fit in a conventional oven. They are simply too big.

I fell corn stalks with a ground ax, leveling the best sweet corn crop we've ever grown. I pull offending raspberry canes free of wet dirt. The plant roots are stubborn and unyielding and I wrench a shoulder in the process. There's no one around so there's no point in complaining.

Jack dances across our lawn in a brand new winter jacket, dress slacks, and new light-up tennis shoes. He's clearly intent on joining me in the garden but his apparel is wholly inappropriate for the task.

"Jack, you need to put on your old jacket and boots," I admonish.

The boy stops in his tracks. Sampson, our fourteen year old yellow Labrador and Daisy, my son Matt's black Labrador-mix, lope behind the child, distracted by their own play.

"I don't wanna."

I'm short on patience. The circumstances of last Friday weigh heavily on my mind as I consider my son.

"Just do it or you'll have to stay inside."

Jack grunts defiance and crosses his arms across his chest. The hood of his new jacket is pulled tight. I can't see Jack's eyes but I know that they're filled with refusal. After an interlude, the child wheels and darts towards the garage. The dogs slide after him. I return to piling dead vegetation in a wheelbarrow. It takes a good half hour to transfer the debris to our compost pile behind the garden shed. By the time the task is completed, Jack is back to playing with the dogs. He's changed his jacket, pants, and shoes, causing me to consider how much he is like his older brother Dylan. Both will complain to high heaven about doing what they're asked to do, only to ultimately comply.

My eyes search the high silver sky for signs of rain or snow. The clouds are insignificant and contain no moisture. If the sky had been like this on Friday, it wouldn't have happened. Tragedy would have been averted. But that wasn't the case. The skies over Eveleth, a small town located on Minnesota's Iron Range, were low and dense with ice. The difference between what's above me now as I work in my vegetable garden and what confronted the Senator's plane is patently obvious.

Though we weren't close friends, I knew Paul Wellstone. I knew his wife more peripherally, as the wife of an energetic United States Senator, as someone I said "hello" to whenever our paths crossed, which wasn't all that often.

The first memory I have of Paul was as an organizer in the Jesse Jackson for President Campaign. René and I took Matt as a little child to see the Reverend Jackson speak at the University of Minnesota-Duluth. The UMD gym, the same locale I saw President John F. Kennedy speak when I was Jack's age, was packed. We were lucky to have tickets. I don't really remember what The Reverend said that day. But I certainly remember Paul Wellstone.

When Wellstone picked up the microphone and challenged all of us in the room to get to work to defeat the Republicans it was as if someone had disturbed a herd of Angus with a cattle prod. There are no words to describe the vitality, the energy, the emotional connection that Paul conveyed on that occasion. It was, and remains for me, through all my years in politics, a singular moment.

Over the years, our paths crossed infrequently. René and I helped host fundraisers for Paul. On several occasions I reminded Senator Wellstone about the need for him to remain true to his populist roots; to remain, in the face of a tide of conservatism and selfishness assaulting the nation, a Liberal. He assured me that he'd never back down, that he'd never yield philosophical ground. And he never did.

Whether you agreed with his politics or not, no one can say that Senator Paul Wellstone wasn't a man of principle. This is best illustrated by his first and last major votes in the United States Senate. When newly sworn in, Paul was called upon to show his support for the United States' invasion of Iraq under the first President Bush. Paul Wellstone opposed that war. He refused to accept that peace was not an option in dealing with Iraq. He voted on his convictions. More recently, in what would turn out to be the last major vote of his career, Senator Wellstone once again refused to yield to the advice of pollsters. In an act of courage and fortitude, against conventional wisdom in a tight re-election campaign, Paul Wellstone refused to support the second war with Iraq. His constituents loved it. His standing in the polls climbed. Integrity, it turns out, does matter.

When my first novel, **The Legacy**, was being printed in the summer of 2000 and I needed folks of prominence to endorse the book, I thought of Senator Wellstone. As I said, we weren't close friends but the moment I asked his staff if he'd take a look at my novel, there wasn't any hesitation. He read it and critiqued it himself, never thinking to assign that task to a staff person. He was the same way with everyone. Whether you were a new judge with a recognizable last name or a retired teacher from Buhl who needed help with medical insurance, the Senator rolled up his sleeves and did what needed to be done.

The tiller churns. My boots are ponderous with soil. No geese fly despite the existence of a hunter's sky. I am careful to till around slumbering carrots, the plants still green despite the advent of hard frost. I avoid tilling up our asparagus plants, a mistake I've made several years in a row. After an hour of following the slowing churning tires of the Troy-Built, our garden is finally at rest. I secure the tiller and other gardening tools in the shed and head towards the banks of the Cloquet River in search of inner calm. I sit at the top of stairs that descend to flowing black water, cloaked in sadness and uncertainty.

I went to church this morning. I prayed for the Wellstone family and for the others who were on the Senator's plane. I'm uncertain that my prayer achieved what I'd intended. Now, as I watch dark water roll past my family's home, I ask God to speak to me. I ask the Great Judge to explain to me why eight innocent people had to perish. I want the Creator to reveal to me why this United States Senator, one of a handful of men possessing the remarkable moral clarity to oppose a war waged solely for personal gain and familial reputation, had to die. But on this Sunday afternoon in Fredenberg Township, Minnesota, I hear nothing but the passing of a slow wind through dead leaves.

Smooth

Winter is once again challenging the order of life for folks who live in the country.

Here it is nearly February and I'm lacing up my old Bauer hockey skates for the first skate of the year. The reason I'm so late in taking to the ice? Last week it was nearly fifty degrees. The Fredenberg ice skating rink, the work of many hours of donated labor by our local volunteer fire department under the careful scrutiny of a part time rink attendant, deliquesced, leaving a pool of brown lake water behind.

Normally, when the ice thaws this late in the season, there is no second chance to skate. But another cold snap stalled over Northeastern Minnesota during the week, allowing the skating rink to be re-flooded in quick fashion.

It's near zero. Jack and I sit in the warming shack. An electric wall heater spits moist warmth into the room. A sixty-watt light bulb emits a halo. I bend over to tighten my son's skate laces.

"This should be fun," I say to Jack as I pull the ends of the strings taut.

"Yep," the child responds curtly, his face buried in the fabric of his hat, his ears and cheeks covered by flaps of fleece-lined nylon.

"That should do 'er," I say, pulling gloves over my hands.

It's an odd year for me. Beginning with my eldest son Matt, who is now twenty-three, I've had a kid playing organized hockey for over sixteen years. No more. Matt was cut from the Hermantown High School team as a sophomore and, for the most part, he hasn't held a hockey stick or laced up his skates in seven winters; the exception being when he played intramural hockey during his first year at Michigan Tech University in Houghton.

Dylan, my second eldest, also felt the unkind blade of the coach's cut this past November. After returning from a tournament in Warroad, Minnesota, Dylan was advised by the head coach, that, after thirteen years of playing hockey for

98

Hermantown, one of only five seniors on the team able to make that claim, his services were no longer needed. As a result of my son's dismissal, I haven't watched a hockey game this season. Not one minute. Not one shift. Not one period.

Christian, my third son, never played the game. His skating shows it. He's a lot like his old man in this respect. I didn't learn to ice skate until I was over thirty, and then only as an adjunct to taking Matt to his practices at the old Hermantown outdoor rink in the days before there was a fancy schmantsy indoor arena.

Jack is five. Given our family's history with the sport, I don't see Jack taking up organized hockey. It's not worth the effort.

But skating for pleasure, with winter tickling your exposed flesh; now that's something worth passing on to a kid. And so, earlier this evening, I asked my youngest son to go to the rink with me.

We walk outside. The sounds of children laughing greet us as we waddle along the rubber path linking the warming house with the ice. I push a chair, a child's chair borrowed from our church, onto the ice. The steel feet of the chair glide across the polished surface of the rink.

"Come on Jack," I urge, pushing the chair towards my son. "Grab onto the back of the chair and walk behind it."

Jack complies and moves forward with unsteady steps. Vapor trails from his mouth. Fathers and children (there are no mothers at the rink on this frigid night) skate lazy circles at the far end of the rink.

"I'll give you a ride," I offer, skating up to Jack, spraying him with shaved ice as I stop sharply.

The boy smiles and takes a seat in the chair. I crouch low and push off with the inside edges of my battered skates. We sail over the ice, the stars and night sky standing visible and clear above the rink's artificial illumination. We pivot around a hockey net, narrowly missing a little girl and her father. Air rushes past us. We gain speed. A bare remembrance of the moon climbs the eastern sky above the darkened land. We circle the far net. I stop. Jack resumes pushing the chair.

One by one, the others depart. Soon, it's only Jack and me and the ice. Cars and trucks come and go at the Minno-ette, a convenience and bait shop located across the road from the warming shack. No one else visits the rink.

"Time to go," I say as I complete an awkward cross-over turn.

"One more ride," the boy pleads.

I search Jack's eyes. I witness in them the hopes of my youngest son and I recall the disappointments of his older brothers. I nod. Jack settles into the chair. I begin to skate. Though the air remains cold, it feels cleansing.

Beanie Babies

It's an annual tradition that I take my sons and my wife to the local Ducks Unlimited Fundraising Banquet. This year, I shelled out nearly two hundred bucks for my wife René, my eighteen year old son Dylan, my five year old son Jack, and myself, to attend. That's just the cost of dinner and our DU memberships. Once we're at the event, we spend more money on raffles and other contests in an attempt to win prizes.

Though we haven't won consistently at these DU events, when we do win, we usually win big. About ten years ago, I won a Stroeger over-under twelve gauge shotgun. When Chris was ten years old, he won a beautiful oak gun cabinet handcrafted by a local cabinet maker. Three years ago, Dylan won a Browning semi-automatic ten gauge goose gun. All told, I figure we're still ahead of the game.

You have to understand that I go to the DU event because it's fun and because DU is a proactive conservation organization. Ducks Unlimited spends millions of dollars each year in the United States, more in Canada, attempting to preserve prairie marshlands and ponds so that waterfowl and wildlife have a place to propagate and perpetuate. Some cynics would say that the only reason DU does what it does is to insure plenty of ducks and geese for the fall hunting season. I don't buy that. The men and women that I've met at these dinners over the years are not just there to support hunting. They're there to preserve clean water, air, and wildlife habitats for all species that live in the marshes and alongside the great waters of North America.

Without the efforts of DU, herons, swans, egrets, and countless other non-game species of birds, not to mention otters, beaver, musk rats, and a myriad of other mammals, would likely disappear from many of the places they are still found.

"Dad, I wanna win somethin'," Jack observed as he followed me from auction table to auction table at the DU dinner.

I was scouting out the silent auction items, placing my name on bid sheets in front of the items I liked.

"OK," I replied. "I think there's a Green Wing table across the room for guys your size."

We walked across the carpeted floor in the Proctor Blackwoods Restaurant and stood in front of the kids' table.

"How much to enter the Green Wing drawing?" I asked a slim older man decked out in western style clothing complete with bolo tie and Stetson.

"Ten bucks a ticket," he replied. "Say, little fella," he continued, looking down at Jack, "you havin' a good time?"

The man tousled Jack's brown hair. The child smiled and nodded.

"I'll take one," I said, handing the man a ten.

The cowboy tore off a ticket and handed it to Jack.

"Put the big end in the drum and keep the little end."

Jack did as he was told. I took the small end of the ticket and tucked it away in my shirt pocket with the other raffle tickets I'd purchased.

Dylan was antsy. There was only one other couple at our table, an elderly psychologist and his wife. It was a Saturday night and my eighteen year old son had places to go, girls to see.

"Dad," Dylan said, wiping the last bit of food away from his mouth, "I'm gonna hit the road. I'll be home by twelve."

"I'll watch your tickets for you," I replied, unwilling to force him to stay any longer. He'd done well to stick it out two hours.

"See ya, Jack," the teenager said as he ambled towards the door. "Win something big."

The slow parade of silent auction items began. The raffles that I'd entered proceeded to conclusion. Despite spending nearly two hundred dollars on tickets, we hadn't won a thing. Finally, we were down to the last event: the Green Wing raffle.

I leaned over to speak with Jack. My instructions were whispered.

102

"Jack, if he pulls your name," I said, pointing to the cowboy at the front of the room, "take the shotgun."

There were seven or eight items to choose from on the Green Wing table. There were nice limited edition prints of dogs and ducks. There was a fishing outfit, complete with rod, reel, and tackle box occupying a corner of the table's covered surface. And there was a gleaming brand new Mossberg twenty gauge semi-automatic junior shotgun resting in the middle of the prizes. The gun was a real gem, worth nearly three hundred dollars.

I glanced around the room. There were only four or five other kids present. Jack had a legitimate shot at winning the gun. My message, though said softly, was said with firmness so that my five year old understood the gravity of his decision.

"Take the gun," I repeated.

Jack's face tilted towards mine. His mouth parted. I strained to hear his acceptance of my direction.

"I want the Beanie Babies."

My eyes darted. The volunteer's hand dipped into a jar filled with tickets. On the Green Wing table behind the cowboy I spotted five small stuffed animals.

"Jack, I'll buy you ten Beanie Babies. Just take the shotgun," I implored.

"And the winner is...Jack Munger."

As we walked through the crowded room other patrons murmured things like:

"Oh, what a cute little boy," and

"Isn't he precious."

I continued my petitions.

"Jack, when we get to the table, take the shotgun."

We stopped in front of the one hundred and fifty or so folks still remaining in the room. I handed the cowboy Jack's ticket.

"What will it be, pardner?" the man said in a *faux* western voice.

My skin began to moisten under my armpits. I bent over to counsel my son.

"Take the friggin' shotgun," I hissed, trying hard to keep the insistence of my words private.

Jack stared at the table. His eyes never focused on the shotgun.

"But I only want just one of the Beanie Babies," he said softly through a pout.

I looked back at René. Her mouth was drawn in a broad smile. She shrugged her shoulders. I was on my own.

"OK," I relented. "He wants the Beanie Babies," I said, gathering the five small stuffed animals into my arms.

Jack's face broke into a broad beam as I handed the animals to him. His feet fairly flew back to our table. The psychologist and his wife chuckled as I sat down, the sting of defeat clearly etched upon my face. Another name was drawn. The second kid was whisked to the front of the banquet hall by his father.

"He'll take the shotgun," the man said, snatching the Mossberg from the table without hesitation.

Back at home later that evening, Christian was appalled to learn about Jack's decision. Instead of debating the issue, Chris ripped the stuffed creatures out of Jack's embrace and raced into my writing study. After five minutes of computer research Chris reentered the great room of our house and tossed the Beanie Babies to the floor.

"Eleven dollars and twenty-five cents," Chris griped. "You passed up a shotgun for eleven dollars and twenty-five cents."

"Relax, Chris," I admonished. "I'm OK with it. Jack told me something that made it easier to accept when we were walking back to the table after he turned down the Mossberg."

"What's that?"

"Well, he looked right at me and said: 'Cheer up dad. You can always buy me a shotgun.'"

Escape

"I'm taking the day off," I announce to René, my wife of twenty-three years.

"For what?"

"For my mental health," I assert. "I haven't been trout fishing all summer. The season ends September 30th. I'd like to put in at least one good day on the water."

My spouse looks at me with understanding eyes. She knows that I am trying to cram a few centuries of living into one human life span. It's a defect in my character that she's come to accept.

"You can't keep adding and adding. You're not going to be able to keep this up," she warns, her words a repetition of countless prior admonitions.

"That's why I need to go brook trout fishing," I explain.

The following morning, I drop my youngest son off at his preschool and head up the North Shore of Lake Superior. I have a list of streams in my head that I want to explore. One in particular stands out. I plan on saving that river for last.

I've admitted it before. I am an inept fly fisherman. I grew up plying the waters of Miller Creek in the Piedmont Heights area of Duluth for native brookies and planted browns using worms for bait. Occasionally, I'd hop on my old Schwinn 5-speed Collegiate, the handlebars and seat modified to effect a touring bike, and pedal to the banks of the Midway River or Keene's Creek in Hermantown. I was a poor fisherman as a teen. I rarely caught trout. I don't want to decrease my chances of success by trying to tempt fish with artificial lures. I remain a worm fisherman and proud of it.

It's a cool, over-cast late summer morning. Despite near perfect conditions for trout fishing, the first two streams I try produce no strikes. I pull into a small grocery store in Finland, Minnesota for a packaged sandwich and a bottle of juice.

"Any luck?" the female cashier, a woman looking to be in her late fifties, asks upon noting my attire.

"Nothing," I say. "But a bad day on the river is better than a good day at the office," I offer, repeating a timeworn cliché.

"That's for sure," she responds, taking my money, making change. "Good luck."

"Thanks," I answer, wandering out the door.

My shins ache. The waders I'm wearing rub just above my ankles where my stockings droop. I pull my socks up over the abrasions, the left ankle more affected than the right, in hopes of preventing further discomfort.

I drive over a logging trail through the bleakness of a Northeastern Minnesota cutover. The loggers have left a meager buffer of timber, mostly aspen and birch, augmented with an occasional pine or spruce, along the streambed. I find a spot where the river, really no more than a creek, passes beneath the gravel road in a culvert. I park my car and pull on my waders.

The socks don't insulate my fractured flesh from the neoprene of the boots. My face grimaces as I pick up my rod, a cheap collapsible spin cast outfit, and ease down the riverbank into the water. Overhead, a flock of several hundred loud Canada Geese swings south. It's too early for the birds to be migrating but not too early for them to be thinking about it.

As I enter the river, I remain concerned. The summer has been unnaturally warm and virtually rainless. These fragile North Shore streams cannot survive without cool, filling rains. I dip my fingers into the lifeblood of the river. It is cold, cold enough to sustain trout. I'm glad. This is my favorite trout stream. I would hate to see it destroyed, the way other local streams have been, by uncontrolled construction of beaver dams that raise the temperature of the headwaters and negatively impact the survivability of speckled trout.

As I struggle through a press of red cedars shading the creek, tossing my hook and worm into places that look like they might hold fish, I marvel at the determination of the Minnesota DNR. Every hundred feet or so, I find evidence that some worker from the State has sliced through logs dropped across the water by intrepid beaver, chain sawing potential logjams out of the way, allowing the river to flow.

It's late afternoon before I land my first brook trout, a small native fish whose flanks sparkle with blue, red, and yellow splashes of color even under the muted sky of the day. I pocket the fish, hopeful that I'll catch more, and continue to struggle downstream, stumbling occasionally over submerged debris and smooth stones as I proceed.

I encounter a quiet pool, the result of rodent engineering. Ahead of me, beaver have managed to string not one, not two, but three dams across the river, slowing the gushing water to a meander. As a fisherman, I recognize that, in the long term, the dams are not beneficial to the health of the stream. But in the short term, I know that larger fish are lurking behind the obstructions.

The banks of the river are undulating mounds of swamp grass, interrupted by shallow pools of standing water and deep canals cut by the beaver. I take a step and watch one leg disappear to the limits of my waders while the other remains affixed to solid ground. Never much good at doing the splits, I extract myself from the deep hole just as water begins to enter my boots.

A red tail hawk glides over the trees. A bluff, its crown covered with spindly pines and undisturbed deciduous trees, rises behind me. A clear-cut looms beyond the timber. I dip my hook and worm into the slow current and wait.

A steady tug. My line disappears from the river's surface. I set the hook into the trout. It's a nice fish; far more powerful than the one I've already taken. The trout seeks refuge in a tangle of roots and dead fall along the far bank of the pond. I horse the fish away from the debris. I ease the brookie towards my waiting hand. The creature breaks the plane of the water. It's a nice ten inch speck. Luminous and vibrant, the fish dances across the water against the cool air. I grasp the fish firmly with one hand, remove the hook from its jaw, and deposit the trout in the game pouch of my vest.

"That's why I'm here," I mutter to myself. "There must be more where that one came from."

Indeed. Several minutes later I latch into a beauty. The strength opposing me is significant. I let the fish glide up and down the pond, carefully keeping it away from dead trees and debris. The brookie finally tires and I pull it from the grip of the river.

"Wow," I muse, studying the powerful flanks of the trout, a specimen over twelve inches in length. A gorgeous catch for any stream. A trophy from the small waters that I'm working.

A few more casts. I snag a log. I pull hard hoping to dislodge the hook. I hear a snap. My cheap collapsible rod breaks apart in unintended fashion.

"Crap," I mutter.

There's nothing left to do. I've caught all the fish I'm supposed to on this day. If one measured the success of the day in dollars, I'm deep in the red. The gas. The lunch. The license. The bait. The rod. All expended for less than a pound of fresh fish. The exchange isn't exactly even.

But that's not how brook trout fishermen, even those that use worms, value things.

The Opener

Thirty-five years. That's how long my father and four of his high school cronies have been spending the Minnesota Fishing Opener at Bob Scott's place on Whiteface Lake north of Duluth. Over that time, there have been many lean years at Whiteface in terms of fish being caught. But fishing isn't why we spend nearly every Mother's Day away from our wives and mothers. Catching fish has very little to do with the Opener.

Before the males in my family ventured up to Scott's cabin for the Opener, we used to fish the Seagull River at the end of the Gunflint Trail. Seagull is a legendary walleye factory. It's where I caught the only truly remarkable walleye I've ever caught. The story went something like this.

You'd motor up the Seagull River under cover of night so you could be at your fishing spot by midnight. At the Narrows, you met up with hundreds of other like-minded folks searching for trophy fish. You'd anchor your boat amidst a raft of other boats and begin fishing. I remember sleeping through most of these late-night gyrations despite my dad's best efforts to keep me excited about the prospect of latching onto a monster walleye.

My big fish wasn't caught anchored in the Narrows. It was hooked while trolling another stretch of the Seagull River in broad daylight. As I recollect, I was still tired from spending the night on the water. I was holding my fishing rod, an old fiberglass cast-off with an open-faced reel, loosely in my hands.

Somewhere along the path we cut through a myriad of other boats, my line went taut.

"Dad, I think I'm snagged," I said.

"That's about par for the course," my father muttered. He was forever untangling my line, baiting my mom's jig with a new minnow, or trying to keep my brother David's hook out of someone's eye. My father is not a patient man.

Putting him in a small boat with three amateurs was always a real test of his mettle.

My father backed the boat up. I tried to reel in the monofilament line but whatever I'd hooked wasn't budging. Then, without warning, my line began to ascend.

"It's coming up," I remarked.

"Probably a stick," my father replied.

I won't belabor the tale. After five minutes of playing the fish, I pulled a ten pound three ounce walleye out of the Seagull River. Though the fish provided little fight and even less excitement, it remains, to this day, the largest fish I've caught. And that walleye was only one of a half dozen fish that we netted during that Opener that exceeded six pounds.

On the Seagull, we were angling over walleye spawning grounds, catching huge females and preventing them from perpetuating their species. This fact wasn't lost upon the Minnesota DNR. Eventually, the State closed the Seagull River to fishing during the Opener. By the time the Seagull was closed, the Munger boys had already started going to the Scott's cabin on Whiteface Lake.

Let me tell you this: Compared to the Seagull River, Whiteface, a slender reservoir lake created by a small dam on the Whiteface River, is the Dead Sea. Oh, every year, the five fathers (we've recently labeled them "The Iron Five" because they're now all over seventy years old) who originated this tradition, brag about years when we caught oodles of walleye and huge northern pike during the Opener. Well, to my memory, if anyone ever caught a limit of fish on Whiteface, it must have been while I was asleep. I can't remember taking more than a handful of nice walleyed pike, fish over three pounds, from the Lake in our thirty-five years of trying.

Our wives, girl friends, and mothers know this to be true. They'd tell you that, despite the fact they've been deserted on most Mother's Days, they've yet to see more than a meager packet or two of walleye fillets come home. This year wasn't any different.

The sky never really cleared. There was near constant drizzle and wind. Fishing was terrible. In my sixteen foot Northland fishing boat, powered by a fifty horse Force outboard, I took, at various times, my father, his pal Red, and my two teenaged sons, Dylan and Chris, across the Lake in search of walleye. We never caught a walleye. Red netted three perch. Dylan caught a northern suitable for a tropical fish tank. My dad, Chris, and I were essentially skunked, unless you count the two slimy snake Northern Pike that Chris reeled in using other people's rods.

It really doesn't matter. The Opener is about eating vast quantities of great food, re-telling old stories, and having a libation or two; though sometimes the two becomes three or more, creating memories that, unfortunately cannot be shared in a family newspaper.

This year, there were twenty-six of us at Bob and Pat Scott's place. For a quarter of a century, Pat Scott has permitted a bunch of carousing fisherman (no daughters, wives, or girlfriends allowed) to invade her lake cottage during the Opener. It's even more astonishing that, for the past ten years, what was once the Scott Cabin, is now the Scott Home. Can you imagine your mother, wife, sister, or daughter putting up with several dozen smelly beer-swilling fishermen in their home for two nights and two days?

We were out on the Lake. The wind finally calmed but clouds and shifting rain remained. Dark shrouded the landscape. I turned the ignition key to start the Force to pull us away from shore. Instead of the satisfying roar of the motor, all I heard was the whining of the starter.

"What the....?" I muttered.

"You remember when that happened last summer, Dad," Christian advised. "You took off the cover and fixed it."

"I did not," I said, certain that I'd never encountered this particular problem with the motor.

I'd already discovered that my trolling motor, a two horse Johnson, was inoperable. I had the thing repaired last summer after Dylan, my muscle-bound son, pulled the recoil rope right out of the unit. His antics broke not only the rope and handle but the recoil spring itself. When I tried to start the motor on Saturday there was no handle and no rope to pull. The shop had replaced the spring but not the handle and rope.

"That happened once last year to Matt and me," Dylan announced.

"You fixed it before too, Dad," Chris insisted.

"I'm telling you that I've never had this motor act like this," I seethed.

"I think your dad would remember if he'd done this before," Grandpa Harry interjected.

"What did Matt do to fix the problem?" I asked as I removed cowling.

"I dunno," Dylan responded.

I muttered something unprintable and fiddled with the armature of the starter. The cog on the starter moved. After further tinkering, I was able to get the starter to connect. The outboard roared to life.

Back at the Scott place on Sunday afternoon, I dig my swimming suit and towel out of my overnight bag. The lake water has been measured by John, Bob and Pat Scott's eldest son, at just over forty degrees. I strip off my clothes, pull on my trunks, and enter the Scott family sauna. Inside, Bob, John, and Joe Scott, (John's son and Bob's grandson) sit on a cedar bench. Wet heat greets my bare skin as I find a place alongside them.

As steam rises off of the rocks, the four of us, one Munger and three generations of Scotts, talk about life, love, politics, and sports. We do not discuss fishing.

Satellite Blues

I'll be the first to admit that I am not a techie. My twenty-two year old son Matthew is. So is my brother-in-law Alan. When the two of them get together and talk, it might as well be in Russian as far as I'm concerned.

Sure, I'm typing this story on a computer. It's the same dinosaur Texas Instruments notebook that I used when I was in private practice as a lawyer. But just because I know how to type on a 486 50MHz piece of history (you thought I was gonna say something else, didn't you?) doesn't mean I know squat about how the thing runs. To me, it's a bit of black magic that my fingers touch the keys and words appear on the screen.

Anyway, Matt came home. He's been away touring the public colleges of the Midwest for three years. He started out as an engineering student at Michigan Tech. Then he migrated to Fargo for a year at NDSU. Now I think he's finally found his niche. He's at the University of Wisconsin-Superior taking courses in business technology systems. A fancy way of saying he's learning how to integrate computers into the business world.

"Dad, we need faster Internet," was one of the first phrases our oldest kid uttered when he came back home to live.

"Why?"

"I'm gonna be downloading all kinds of assignments from my professors and I'll need to be able to do it quickly."

"We don't have access to fiber optics or cable out here," I advised.

We live on the banks of the Cloquet River twenty miles from town. Where we live, we're lucky we have telephone service. Given this reality, I thought the issue of high speed Internet was dead. Unfortunately, I didn't figure on two techies putting their heads together.

"Alan, what do you know about satellite Internet?" Matt asked when my brother-in-law was at our house for Christmas.

Alan works in the Twin Cities for a technology company. I've never really understood what he does. When he's around Matt, there's precious little conversation about such details.

"Funny you should ask," Alan responded. "I bought a new dish for work. I was going to use it at one of remote sites in Ohio but I haven't tried it yet. I'd be willing to haul it up here and let you try it to see if it works. If it does, you can just buy it from the company. If it doesn't, I'll take it down."

"Dad?"

I feigned deafness. My deception didn't last.

A Saturday morning in early February. I'm waiting for Alan, his wife Colleen, and their two little kids to arrive. I'm slated to assist my brother-in-law with the installation of the satellite dish.

"Where are you going to put that thing?" René asks as she wanders into the kitchen. "I don't want some ugly satellite dish standing out like a sore thumb in the front yard," she adds.

"Alan needs to aim it to the southwest. The front yard is the best place to put it. It's gonna be on a wooden pallet. It's only temporary."

René's look is stern.

"It's not going to be standing in my front yard," is all she says between sips of strong coffee.

Later that morning, my wife's instruction clear in my mind, Alan and I lug a pallet towards the back of the house as we discuss a location for the temporary installation.

"Can we put it off the three season room in the back? It'll have a clear shot over the pasture to the southwest?"

"That'll work," Alan responds.

Despite the fact that he's a techie, I genuinely like Al, though I've never called him that. I've never asked him if he'd respond to Al rather than Alan. Probably not. Alan suits him.

114

"Twenty-three," I call out over one of Alan's walkie-talkies.

The dish is positioned precariously on the pallet, pointed between two gigantic white pines off to the southwest. I gave Alan a woodsman's approximation of southwest. My brother-in-law insisted on checking the orientation with a GPS. Turns out my instincts were within a degree of true southwest: A triumph for man over machine.

Alan is outside with another radio wiggling the dish up and down and from side to side in an attempt to increase the percentage of connection to the computer from twenty-three percent to something over thirty-five percent, the minimum required to get a useable signal. Despite the fact that it's February and windy, it's not cold. This is not a job you'd want to be doing in below zero weather. Not that I'm shivering. I'm sitting behind a keyboard in Matt's bedroom. My sole job is to relay numbers from the computer screen to Alan via the walkie-talkie.

I don't want you to think that there wasn't debate as to whether Matt's personal computer or our home computer, located in Christian's room, should be hooked up to the satellite dish. There was considerable discussion of that topic amongst our three oldest boys. But in the end, given that Matt was the one who "needed" a faster Internet connection, the cable is being brought into his room.

Alan and I work throughout the morning trying to increase the satellite signal. By 1:30pm, when it's time for lunch, we've actually gone backwards.

"I don't know why we can't get a better connection," my brother-in-law laments between bites of hot pizza.

"Maybe it's just not gonna work."

"We're missing something. It'll work," Alan promises.

Matt comes home from his job and I escape further involvement in the project. Before abdicating my role, I leave my eldest son with a parting bit of advice.

"It's never gonna work."

For the remainder of the day, I am smugly satisfied. Instead of increasing the percentage of connection between the computer and satellite, the number plummets further.

115

Finally, even Alan admits defeat. My wife diverts his attention from the Internet project to wiring under-the-counter lights in our kitchen. That project turns out to be an overwhelming success.

"Sorry it didn't work," Alan mutters as he steps away from our front porch. It's near nightfall and the Schostags are headed back to the Twin Cities.

"Not your fault," I say, trying to conceal my "I told you so" glee.

Later in the evening, René and I go out to dinner with friends. Matt enlists his brother Chris to monitor the computer screen. My eldest son mounts the dish to the wooden posts supporting our three-season room and manipulates the unit in search of a better signal. My wife and I arrive home around midnight. We hear voices in the basement.

"I've tried that," Matt advises to someone over the telephone. He's a true techie. He's wearing a headset, his cell phone strapped to his waist, as he walks around the room. "That too," he continues.

"How's it going?" I ask as I enter his bedroom.

I note that that graph on the computer monitor shows a twenty-three percent connection to the satellite, exactly the same number that Alan and I obtained when we first turned the thing on at ten o'clock that morning.

"I'm on the phone with Hughes," my eldest son admonishes, naming the manufacturer of the ill-fated dish.

"Dad, I wanna go to bed," Christian laments through an open window. My third son peers into Matt's bedroom from outside. His face betrays that he's cold, tired, and fed-up with his older brother.

"You're not any further along, are you?"

Matt ignores me.

"Ten more minutes and then let Christian go to bed," I warn.

My eldest continues to talk on the phone.

Fifteen minutes pass. I crawl into bed. René is in the bathroom brushing her teeth. I hear a blood-curdling cry from the bowels of the basement. I leave the comfort of our king-sized platform and pad down the stairs.

"What's up?" I ask Matt.

"I can't believe it," my eldest boy says.

"Can't believe what?"

"Alan."

"What about Alan?"

"I asked him about the little labels covering the ends of the dish receiver. He said they wouldn't make any difference. The guy at Hughes asked if I'd taken them off. I asked why. He said the dish won't work with the labels on."

"You're kidding, right?"

My son beams. His eyes are heavy with fatigue but his face clearly betrays an "I told you so" look.

"Check it out. I took the covers off and the thing jumped to sixty-eight percent. I'm logged on to MSN right now."

The graph on the computer screen proves the obvious and it's my turn to eat crow.

Ron's Turtle

My neighbor Ron has only one hand and only part of his left arm. The details of how and why he lost part the limb aren't important to this story. The fact that Ron, in a very limited sense, is physically challenged, is relevant to this tale.

A couple of summers ago, René and I were visiting Ron and Nancy's motor home on Island Lake. The details of why we were there aren't significant. I remember it was a cloudy Saturday during the summer and that lots of other folks were milling around the place, enjoying the hospitality of the McVeans. Beyond that, only limited recollections of the day remain vivid in my mind.

I was trying to play horseshoes. I say trying because I consider myself to be lawn game challenged. With the exception of volleyball, where I can use determination to compensate for my lack of athleticism, I'm pretty much a failure at your standard picnic games.

Thud.

More often than not, the horseshoe would land on the grass great distances from its intended target. Sometimes the projectiles would turn sideways in the air and land on the run, rolling hell-for-leather towards innocent bystanders. Only once out of every hundred or so throws did I hit the stake. Only once out of every thousand tosses did the horseshoe catch the post and complete a ringer.

Ron was absent from the game. He usually supervises my ineptitude by offering gentle pointers such as:

"You throw like a girl, Munger."

Or:

"Didn't you ever play this game growing up?"

But Ron wasn't by my side as I launched ponderous metal objects into the summer sky.

"What 'cha doin'?" I asked when I caught up with Ron later that afternoon.

My friend appeared deeply immersed in a task. He was sitting on his dock. Tannin-stained water lapped the aluminum sides of the wharf. A pair of mallards floated contentedly as a small breeze worked up a walleye chop. Ron appeared dedicated to some small task. He didn't look up as he responded.

"I'm trying to fillet this darn turtle."

The rough shell of a snapping turtle was secured under the stump of Ron's left arm. The animal was obviously dead.

"Why?"

"I want turtle soup," Ron advised. "This critter was eating the fish on my stringer and wouldn't let go when I picked him up so I whacked off his head with a hatchet."

My friend raised the heavy reptile with his good hand and beamed proudly.

"She's a big one," I said, guessing from the size of the reptile that it was a female.

"Should be good eating," Ron offered.

"Ever tried it?" I asked dubiously.

"Nope, but I hear it's good."

To make the record clear, despite the fact that Ron has only part of his left upper appendage, I've learned over the years that there are very few things Ronald McVean cannot do when he puts his mind to it. He's bested me at one-on-one basketball. He's slammed a volleyball down my throat on any number of occasions. He's good with tools, better with computers, and recently wired the entirety of his new house. But that day, watching Ron struggle to hold the snapper under the remnant of his left arm while trying to cut into the thick undercarriage of the turtle with a fillet knife, it seemed to me that my friend could use some help.

Still, offering aid to a person with an obvious physical impairment isn't something one does cavalierly. I weighed the fact that Ron is a proud and hard-working man, someone who has not let a little detour on life's road impact his love of life, his God, and his family, against the fact that he wasn't making much progress cutting up the critter.

"Want some help?"

There wasn't any hesitation.

"You bet. I can't hold the thing and cut at the same time."

Though I'd never dissected a turtle, my high school biology experiences having been limited to cats, frogs, and fetal pigs, it didn't look all that tough for someone with two functioning hands to cut the meat away from the shell of a dead reptile.

The sun came out. The day grew long. Ron wandered off to entertain his guests. I sawed away at the unforgiving sinew of the turtles' musculature. Deer flies and horse flies appeared, teased into activity by the hot sun. My progress was continually interrupted as I swatted insects trying to burrow into my scalp. I cut my thumb trying to slice and swat at the same time. Thick crimson blood flowed from the wound bathing the turtle in red.

"I need a band aid," I yelled.

One of my kids located a bandage in Ron and Nancy's motor home. I protected the wound and worked on.

Dinner hour came. Ron reappeared with a plastic baggie for the turtle meat; lean, red muscle that looked a little like beef but smelled like chicken droppings.

"Is that all the farther you are?"

"Shut up," I said, half annoyed, half amused that my dissection of a dead animal had consumed the better part of a beautiful summer day.

"You don't have to get testy."

"This is a lot harder than it looks."

"Looks like we'll have enough for soup."

After two and half-hours of diligent effort, the shell was finally clean of flesh.

"Cool," Ron said, hanging the protective covering of the turtle on a nearby birch limb. "The birds can pick off the rest."

My thumb stopped bleeding. I removed the bandage and washed my hands in the lake. Ron's wife Nancy walked onto the dock.

"Ronald, what are you going to do with that?" she said, pointing to the bag of turtle pieces in my friend's right hand.

"Put it in the freezer. Some winter night we'll invite Mark and René over for turtle soup."

"That stuff will sit in our freezer forever. You're never going to make turtle soup."

"That's it," I exclaimed, rinsing my hands in the cool lake water of Island Lake. "Where do you want the guts?"

"Put 'em over there," Ron responded, pointing to a weedy area along the shoreline some distance from the revelry. "The gulls can eat 'em."

"They'll stink to high heaven," Nancy objected.

"Put 'em over there," Ron commanded once more.

I did as I was told.

Years intervened. The McVean's built a beautiful home on their lake lot. In the process of moving, Nancy discovered the turtle meat congealed as a disgusting lump at the bottom of the family deep freeze. Ron was away at work when his wife removed the hard-won gains of my reptilian autopsy and tossed the mess into the garbage.

Floating

There is water everywhere. It has rained like cats and dogs for weeks. The past month has seen only brief interruptions in the precipitation. Those days without moisture have, with rare exception, been unnaturally cold.

Pewter clouds roll overhead as I set the bow of my Grumman square stern canoe in the waters of the Cloquet River. Bleak water rushes beneath the aluminum watercraft. I am determined to fish the River. It's Memorial Day weekend. I should be up North, in the Boundary Waters Canoe Area with my three oldest boys, enjoying a pristine wilderness experience. But I am not.

Matt, my eldest, was the first to break the news to me.

"Hi Dad. About this weekend..." he related over the telephone.

"Huh huh," I responded.

"I have to work."

"Matt," I admonished my eldest, "I've had the permit for months. You've known about the trip since January."

"I know Dad. They want me to work. They're short-handed. I can't turn them down. I can't pass up the time and a half. I need the money."

A wave of upset rose inside of me. I tried to maintain a calm demeanor. I couldn't very well fault the kid for trying to put some money the bank. After all, he was paying his own way in college after two years on the "Munger Scholarship Plan" at Michigan Technological University.

"Fine."

"Fine" is such an interesting word. Paradoxically, the phrase generally denotes situations where things are anything but "fine".

"Don't be upset, Dad."

"I'm not."

"Yes you are. I can tell."

Of course, he was right. I let my anger cool.

"How about trying some brown trout fishing if I can find some time later this summer?" I asked, thinking of a well-known river not too far from where my eldest son was living at the time.

"Sure."

I let it go at that. The same night I had virtually the same conversation with Dylan, my second son.

"Dad, I can't go this weekend."

Lucky for Dylan, Matt had already softened my resolve.

"Gotta work?"

"Yep."

There was no apology from my egocentric teenager. René, my wife, a professional therapist, advised that a voluntary apology is unlikely from any teenager. In the process of mollifying my discontent, René pointed out that adolescents are human beings instilled with an infallible belief that the universe revolves around them.

"OK," I responded.

That left Chris, my thirteen year old and me. I knew that René and Jack, our three year old, weren't interested in fighting the forecast; prolonged rain and cold. Under ordinary conditions, my wife would be more than willing to tromp around the BWCA but she wasn't about to volunteer to do it in the pouring rain.

"Dad, Curtis wants me to go camping with him."

One of Christian's classmates asked if Chris could go with his family to Wisconsin for Memorial Day Weekend. The request came as I was contemplating whether or not the two of us should venture up to Brule Lake in the BWCA. My son's intense brown eyes reflected a clear desire to go with Curtis.

"Fine."

Funny how that word seemed to roll off my tongue and linger naturally in the air.

I pull the recoil on the little Johnson two horse to make sure that the motor will start. The outboard coughs. A cloud of blue exhaust spits into the cool air. The fuel ignites and the canoe surges through the water. I shut the outboard down. I'll need the engine for the return trip. For the trip down river, the natural flow of the River is sufficient to move the canoe along.

At intervals during my drift, I toss lures into locations that normally produce game fish. I manage to hook and land a three-pound sucker. Nothing else bites. Several pairs of wood ducks, the males resplendent in their plumage, rise from the river and scurry out of my path. I munch on Ritz crackers and sip bottled root beer while I fish. Stray raindrops tumble from the sky and strike the slick rubber of my raincoat as the canoe floats along. There isn't enough precipitation to make me run for cover; just enough to make me wet and uncomfortable.

I drift through a series of modest rapids and come to rest in a flat pool. I cast and cast and cast but nothing strikes the floating jig head and dew worm I offer. I scan the shoreline for signs of nature. No deer appear. No rabbits scurry beneath the bramble. No beaver plow through the water.

My stomach rumbles. It's past dinnertime. Chris is somewhere in Wisconsin, splashing in the pungent water of a chlorinated campground swimming pool. Matt is hoisting and carrying boxes at work. Dylan is keeping a close watch on plumbing supplies.

I start the motor and begin the short journey home. In a matter of seconds, the sky opens up.

Indian Lake

The Lumina bounced along the blacktop highway north of Pequaywan Lake. Matt, my eldest son, sat in the front passenger seat. Christian, my third son, occupied the seat behind me as I drove.

"This seems like an awfully long ways," Chris noted. "You sure we can do this trip in four days?"

"The map says..."

"Oh no, not the map thing again," Matt lamented.

"You got somethin' against reading a map before you go on a canoe trip?" I asked.

"It's not *that* you read the map, Dad, it's *how* you read the map that concerns me," my eldest son replied.

I remained quiet, unwilling to enter into a debate at eight o'clock in the morning heading into the weekend. The forest, a mixture of evergreens, aspen, and birch, slipped by. Finally, the sign I'd been looking for loomed ahead.

"Here we are," I said as I made a left turn onto a gravel road.

We were to begin our paddle on the Upper Cloquet River at Indian Lake, a dime-sized pocket of water attached to the river and located near Brimson, Minnesota. Matt was along to drive the van home once Chris and I launched our canoe. Home was our target. Because our house sits on the banks of the Cloquet River a mile and a half below the Island Lake Dam, it was my vision (hopefully not a nightmare) to canoe from Indian Lake, forty to fifty miles north of our property, down the Cloquet, through Alden Lake, back into the Cloquet, and then, with one final rush of enthusiasm, across the nine mile length of Island Lake. At the western end of Island Lake, we'd portage the Minnesota Power dam, drop the canoe back into the river, and finish the trip, ending up right in front of our house.

A cold Lake Superior wind greeted us as we exited the van. Matt and I flipped the canoe off the vehicle and left it next to the lakeshore for Chris to load. I took a deep breath of fresh country air and admired the scenery as Chris piled duffel bags and fishing equipment into the bottom of the battered Coleman canoe.

"Good luck," Matt said as he stood next to the driver's door of the van watching the Coleman float free of the sandy bottom of Indian Lake.

"It'll be nice if the wind keeps coming from the east," I replied.

Matt entered the Lumina and slammed the door. The van's tires spun in the gravel before propelling the Chevrolet behind trees. My attention shifted. I searched the lake's shoreline for the outlet to the River.

"The channel's over there," Chris said, pointing to a funnel of water jutting south.

"You're wrong." I said with confidence, aiming for another bay.

My guess turned out to be a dead end. Chris was right. Thankfully, he didn't chastise my navigational skills as we edged into the slow current of the river after paddling an extra ten minutes.

The Cloquet River begins its descent from Indian Lake as a series of winding manipulations through high sand banks. White pine, spruce, jack pine, and an assortment of broad leafed trees shelter the watercourse.

"What are those?" Chris asked as we slid by one of the sand banks just outside Indian Lake.

"Turtles."

"There must be fifty of 'em."

"They're wood turtles. They're rare, only find 'em on the upper reaches of the Cloquet."

We pulled up to shore to investigate. The reptiles were indeed wood turtles, lounging in the intermittent sun, preparing nests. Chris crawled out of the canoe, hoisted a specimen to confirm my observation, and gently placed the turtle back on the loose sand.

"That was neat," Chris said as we pushed away from the bank.

After several hours of paddling we arrived at the first portage. In high water it appeared that the rapids ahead of us could be run. But, due to the water conditions, there was no way a kayak, much less a fully loaded canoe, could make it through the narrow passage.

Chris and I donned our caps and began unloading the Coleman. A man appeared from somewhere down the trail. He was old and doubled over with some malady but his eyes sparkled as he spoke.

"Headed downriver?"

"To our house below the Island Lake dam," I replied.

"Water was a lot higher last week."

"You ever catch any fish around here?" I asked between loads.

"Walleyes, northern, crappies, and the occasional brown," the old man said, squinting at me as he took in my face.

"Really. I thought there were supposed to be brookies up this way."

"Browns. The water's perfect for fishing right now. It was too high for the Opener."

I asked some more questions, mostly about the landscape beyond the first rapids and the locations of campsites further downstream. The old man confirmed that there was a formal campsite complete with fire ring and primitive latrine just below the rapids we were skirting.

Chris and I passed the campsite as we drifted below the rapids we had portaged. Since it was too early in the day to make camp, we pushed on.

The landscape reminded me of the lower river. Slow current and dark water sliced between low rounded banks strangled with pines, birch, balsam, and aspen. Towards dusk, we scared up a muskrat. Evidence of beaver was everywhere in the piles of slashings, felled trees, and impressive habitations.

"See that little pool?" I asked Chris as we rounded a sharp corner. "According to the map, there should be a campsite here."

Chris muttered something about maps but didn't voice any serious opposition to checking out the shoreline. We found a neatly cleared campsite, complete with fire ring, cooking grate, latrine, and a ready supply of cut firewood exactly where the map said it should be.

After setting up the tent, starting a campfire, and eating a dehydrated meal cooked in a pouch, my son pulled out a traveling chess board, opened it on a balsam stump, and began placing the pieces in their appropriate squares.

"Wanna play?" Chris asked as I finished the last of the dinner dishes.

"Sure," I replied. "I'll kick your butt."

A propane lantern hissed noisily from its perch on a flat rock as we sat on folding camp chairs plotting our moves. The day departed. Velvet settled over the campsite as I achieved checkmate.

Morning broke on the river. Mist rose from cold water and merged with warming air. I awoke from the sort of desperate slumber gained when one sleeps on rocky ground. Age is not kind to canoeists. One's ability to sleep on a thin pad of foam does not increase over time.

Chris was still asleep as I filled steel camping pots with river water, started the single burner propane stove, and cooked breakfast. Instant oatmeal, hot cocoa, tang, and hot coffee were soon ready.

"Get up," I urged. Chris didn't stir inside the tent.

"Time for breakfast," I repeated.

There was a slight moan in reply. I sat on a stump and ate my cereal. A beaver cruised upstream passing a spot where I'd encountered a set of timber wolf tracks imprinted along the shore. The tracks went right through our camp following those of a small deer. I wondered about the drama that likely unfolded between hunter and prey somewhere downstream.

Slap.

The beaver detected my presence and gave warning to its companions. Chris climbed out of his sleeping bag, donned his clothes, and joined me. In short order, we finished breakfast, cleaned the dishes, and packed the canoe for the second day of our trip.

We entered a slow, meandering portion of the Upper Cloquet River that can best be described as maple savanna.

The inconsequential banks of the River were defined by tall grass and spindly maple trees. Gone were the high bluffs and conifers that marked the beginning of our trek. White pines and red pines were visible on the horizon but did not crowd the water. A white tail deer, its fur muted amber against the morning sun, browsed marsh grass along the bank in front of us before sauntering off into the trees.

Our progress halted. Beaver had successfully bridged the Cloquet River by dropping a massive oak tree as an anchor for a dam in progress.

"Looks like a good place to have lunch," I remarked. "We'll have to portage around the beaver dam anyway."

"Sounds good," Chris responded.

The muddy banks surrounding the dam were steep. It took great effort to drag the fully loaded canoe up the incline and onto flat ground. Evidence of beaver infestation was everywhere.

"Look at all the beaver crap," I said, my feet mired in ooze.

"Gross," my son responded.

After finding a patch of ground clear of beaver leavings, we ate lunch before portaging around the beaver dam. Once on the water, we resumed paddling the unremarkable stretch of floodplain. I tossed a spinner and a night crawler along the shore. No fish took the offering. Chris slept soundly in the sunshine as we floated. A stiff wind out of Manitoba prevented warmth.

"Another portage," I said as the Coleman rounded a lazy bend. "Must be getting close to Alden Lake," I surmised. I didn't bother confirming our location on the map. We had ample daylight left and we weren't in a hurry.

The sound of a four-wheeler rumbling through the woods greeted us as the bow of our canoe struck land. A Polaris ATV, the driver, heavy set and circumspect, pulled into view.

"Where you headed?" the man asked.

"To our house on the Lower Cloquet," I replied, climbing over a Duluth Pack and a stack of duffle bags in the middle of the Coleman. "We started at Indian Lake."

"Water's down," the man responded.

We inspected the portage. The guy sat on his vehicle, his ample belly covered by a "Minnesota Vikings" pullover, as he reflected on the churning whitewater.

"Doesn't look so bad," I related as we viewed the rapids from a rocky point. "Wanna try?"

Chris looked at the water. His eyes focused on an ominous portion of the plunge.

"What about that?" he said, pointing to a rocky ledge and narrow plume of water spouting between two gigantic boulders.

"I think we can slide between the rocks," I offered. "It'll be tight, but if we crank it to the left as soon as we come over the lip, I think it's doable."

Gray cloaked the afternoon. The sun had vanished. A chill infiltrated my clothing as I walked back to our canoe.

"Well?" I asked again.

"Sure," the teenager responded.

"You gonna try 'er?" the stranger asked as he pulled alongside our canoe on his ATV. "My son does it all the time in higher water. He's never done it this low."

"I think we'll give it a whirl," I replied, climbing back into the Coleman.

"Good luck," the man offered without conviction.

We paddled across the river and sat quietly in the last bit of calm water above the rapids. I studied the rocky ledge, looking for an entry point that wouldn't leave us hung up. The last thing I wanted to do was get stuck on a rock.

"Ready?" I asked.

"Yep," Christian responded.

"Just keep your paddle in the canoe until I ask for help," I reminded my son. "Let me steer. If you put out your paddle before I tell you to, we'll likely end up sideways on a rock."

Chris didn't respond. I assumed my son heard my admonition.

The entirety of the Cloquet River was gathered in the flume descending between the two boulders. There was no water to the right of the ledge: only additional boulders and

130

shallows. To the left, the water thinned out until it was only a few inches deep, making travel by canoe impossible.

"Here we go," I shouted.

Gravity grabbed the canoe. Spires of water rose around us. A boulder loomed above us. I dug deep on the left side of the stern and tried to pivot away from the rock. The canoe didn't respond.

In a panic, Chris stuck out at the rock with his paddle. The shift in my son's weight caused the canoe's left gunwale to dip into the water. The River poured into the bottom of the Coleman.

"Don't reach," I shouted. "Keep your paddle inside the canoe until I tell you otherwise."

There was an instant, as water surged over the plastic edge of the canoe, when I thought we were going to swamp. But Christian shifted his weight back to center and I dug hard against the current. The change was enough to right the craft. The canoe slid through the narrows.

"All right," I shouted, raising my paddle in triumph as the Coleman shot into the flats below the flume.

"That was something," Chris noted.

"Paddle," I shouted, angling the canoe across the shallows.

The bottom of the canoe bounced and slid across rocks as we continued downstream.

"Look," Chris said, pointing towards the left shoreline.

The big man sat expressionless on the ATV watching our progress. It was obvious that he'd selected his vantage point in hopes of witnessing disaster. I was happy to disappoint him. He waved half-heartedly as we passed by.

"Oh, oh," Chris moaned.

"What?"

"There's more."

Another set of rapids, a complication not apparent from our former vantage point on the trail, loomed ahead of us. We passed through the second barrier without incident.

Afternoon grew into evening. I heard the sounds of an outboard motor up ahead.

"We must be getting close to Alden Lake."

"You said that two hours ago," my tired son reminded me.

"Ya, but this time, I really mean it," I teased.

We passed the intersection of the Little Cloquet River and the main Cloquet River. The channel widened. The watercourse took on the attributes of a lake. Rounding a bend, a pontoon boat came into view. It was the first boat or canoe we'd seen in two days. Two men worked on an old outboard motor in the middle of the channel trying to get the engine to idle. Blue exhaust drifted against the pewter sky. We paddled past the floating rig. One of the guys, his sweatshirt covered in motor oil, raised his hand in a slight wave. I nodded. We pushed on.

OK, so I got us lost on Alden Lake. I know what you're thinking. Alden Lake, a relatively modest bulge in the Upper Cloquet River, is too small to get lost on. Well, that might be true if you're simply looking to stay on the lake. But if you're searching for the Lake's outlet to the Cloquet River, it isn't that hard to get turned around.

"Dad, why are we paddling back where we came from?" Chris asked as we wandered around Alden Lake.

"I messed up," I confessed.

"But you're the guy with the map," he quipped.

I didn't respond. I simply paddled.

Eventually, we found our way into the river and camped on a small island just below the outlet from Alden Lake. During the night, a thunderstorm rolled in from the west. Though the bad weather only lasted half an hour or so, the force of the wind was remarkable. Our small dome tent, sitting as it was on a small island in the middle of the River, was unprotected from the gale. As rain descended the wind increased until it sounded like a freight train lumbering across a railroad crossing. The thin fabric of our shelter billowed and lifted off the ground constrained only by tent pegs thrust into shallow soil and the weight of two terrified campers.

"I hope it holds," I whispered as the tent rocked and pitched in the storm. There was no response from my son.

Dawn came quietly to the River. The clouds were gone when I left my sleeping bag to start the propane stove for coffee. A pair of wood ducks flew above the far bank of the stream. The sun had not yet climbed into the eastern sky but the day was already beginning to warm. The tent had held. We had stayed dry. All in all the experience had been, to use a common adjective used by today's teens, "awesome."

Below the island we ran numerous riffles and small rapids without incident. The landscape became familiar. The flat savanna that we'd negotiated gave way to terrain nearly identical to that surrounding our home. Pines and balsams became prevalent. The river channel began to feature boulders, rocks, and ledges as its pitch increased.

Late in that morning we encountered significant rapids. We beached the canoe and scouted the turbulence.

"Looks doable," I said, noting that the rapids were moderate. "We'll have to pull like hell to make it from the top section across to that chute," I noted, pointing to a tight passage near the middle of the rapids. "But I think we can make 'er."

"Let's go," Chris agreed. "I don't want to portage."

It was the fastest water we'd run. The bottom of the Coleman never touched a rock as we blew through the first flurry, pulled hard across the current, found a passage and scooted down a second series of riffles before the river spit us past an island in the middle of the channel.

"That was a hell of a paddle," a guy commented from the comfort of a canvas camping chair on the island. A group of five men, the first canoeists we'd seen on the trip, nodded approvingly as we drifted by their campsite. "You made it look easy," the guy added as he sipped hot coffee from a tin cup, the steam of the beverage obvious against fragile morning light.

I nodded. The current pulled us away. The Coleman slid easily through other riffles and rapids. The stream's speed began to increase as we neared Island Lake, a large reservoir lake holding water for Minnesota Power's hydroelectric system. Chris and I had canoed this stretch of the Upper Cloquet when my Uncle Willard, a state representative involved with environmental preservation, led a group of legislators and conservationists down the river.

Three bald eagles left their perches and soared overhead, appearing to race us to the lake.

"I don't think we can portage that mess," I advised as we scrutinized the water just above Island Lake. "There's no channel."

"Time to portage," Chris reluctantly agreed.

The portage trail was rutted and muddy from rain. We made several trips across the slippery path transporting our gear to the lower end of the rapids.

Bathed in brilliant late morning sunlight we ate peanut butter and jelly on soft shell tortillas, drank Kool-Aid, and munched beef jerky for trail lunch. Water coursing over rock provided a noisy backdrop as we filled our bellies with food and our souls with beauty. Across the water, two nylon dome tents rustled in the breeze.

"The wind will be in our faces when we hit the Lake," I noted. "I guess we'll just have to deal with it."

Chris nodded as he fought with the tough beef.

The Coleman slid over the boulders demarcating the border of river and lake without incident. Fishing boats bobbed in the lake. We were no longer alone on our journey. We were back in the 21st century, surrounded by outboard motors, jet skis, and year-round lake homes.

The wind was strong. Despite the steady breeze and white-capped waves, Chris was a trooper. He never whined or complained as we plodded across open water. "Let's have dinner at Porky's," I said as we passed beneath the Island Lake Bridge, my arms tired, my legs cramped from two hours of paddling.

"I'll go for that," Chris agreed.

We beached the canoe and made our way up to the highway. A short walk on blacktop brought us to Porky's Drive-in, a throw-back to the 1950's: a vintage roadside restaurant where you order your food at an outside counter and eat at tables under open sky.

"I was thinking," I offered between bites of well-done cheeseburger and onion rings, "that maybe we should surprise

Mom and come home a day early. If we keep paddling, we can probably be across the lake before evening. It's only a mile and a half down river to the house from there," I observed.

"OK," Chris agreed, his mouth full of burger, grasshoppers audible in the near distance.

The wind hadn't lessened any by the time we ventured back onto the lake. With little discussion we paddled across another five miles of open water with whitecaps rolling beneath the plastic bottom of the canoe. I was thankful that we'd taken the Coleman. It's the only one of our three canoes with a keel. In surging waves, even an inch of raised plastic running down the spine of a canoe can be significant. A keel keeps the craft on line between dips of the paddle making course corrections less frequent.

"I think that's the bay we turn into to get to the dam," I said optimistically.

"I'm not sure," Chris said, his mistrust of my navigational skills obvious. "I think it's further down."

The kid was right. We had another mile to paddle. As we approached land the shoreline on either side of the dam was cluttered with humankind.

It was clear from water stains on the concrete portion of the dam that Island Lake was five to six feet below its normal water level. I'd suspected that this was the case. As we'd passed through the lake, we'd seen pontoon boats resting on extended beaches and docks that didn't come close to reaching water. The meager rain of the past evening had not made a dent in the drought. It would take a storm of Noah-like proportions to bring the lake's level back to normal.

I portaged the canoe across the dam and down a steep rocky slope before resting the watercraft on a gravel beach. As Chris and I lugged our gear down the same path, brown skinned Native American children flitted through newly leafed aspen trees playing exhausting games of tag while their parents fished from shore. Other anglers stood waist deep in the water wearing chest waders, tossing spinners and jigs towards the dam's outlet. The water exiting the dam foamed, accentuating the illusion that the Lower River was a giant vat of root beer. We loaded our canoe and slipped into the current.

Water frothed. The plastic bottom of the Coleman bounced off boulders as we slid easily through the rapids below the dam. Mallards and teal escorted us as we paddled home. The concrete bridge over the Taft Road loomed ahead. We passed into shadow and floated by our old farmhouse, the place that originally drew our family to the Cloquet River. As we drifted downstream towards our new home, the voices of my wife and my youngest son Jack echoed across the water. A yellow sun dipped in the west just above hills marking a familiar bend in the river.

"René," I shouted, "we're here."

My wife appeared at the top of the riverbank.

"You're home early," she said.

"We thought we'd surprise you," Chris advised.

An unfamiliar yip broke the quiet interlude as we landed the canoe. The furry head of a yellow Labrador puppy appeared next to my wife at the top of the slope.

Yip.

Jack materialized from behind his mother. The puppy cocked its head and took a defensive stand as if to protect my wife and my youngest son.

"Meet your new dog," René advised.

Transitions

The trial lasted six days. Even though being the judge on a complex civil case isn't as taxing for the judge as it is for the lawyers, there's still a certain amount of stress that makes its presence known by the end of a long case. I was ready for respite. I was ready for the North Shore of Lake Superior.

"Remember, I'm taking Friday off," I reminded my wife René on Wednesday as we cleaned up after dinner. "I think I'll head up the Shore to do some trout fishing, maybe bring a shotgun with, take Copper for a walk in the woods."

"I have an appointment Friday morning. I guess I'll have to get someone to watch Jack," my wife answered, referencing our youngest son.

I was happy she didn't try to talk me into foregoing the trip. She seemed to know that I needed a day for myself.

6:00am came early. The alarm sounded. I forced my eyes open, stumbled through the darkness of our bedroom, and ran a hot shower. The Lumina was already loaded with my waders, a fly rod, my fishing vest, rain gear, Grandpa Jack's side-by-side .410, and a box of thirty year old Number 7 shells. Dressed in blue jeans, a heavy fleece shell, and wool socks, I rambled to the basement level.

"Dylan, time to get up," I hollered through my second son's closed door. "It's six thirty," I advised.

There was no answer.

"Dyl," I repeated with emphasis.

"Wake Chris up," was the response, "he needs to take his shower first."

I stepped to the next door.   "Christian," I yelled, "time to get up."

There was a low moan from my third son in reply. I left the basement, walked into the cool dark of the garage and loaded a travel kennel into the back of the van for our five month old yellow lab pup.

"Here, Copper," I yelled. "Here boy!"

The pup pranced into the garage. An open door revealed the ascending light of a new day. It was going to be sunny and clear, a great day to hunt partridge: not so great a day to catch brook trout. Copper leaped into the kennel without hesitation. I shut the cage's wire door and closed the van's hatch. Sampson, our old yellow lab, a dog decrepit with arthritis, hard of hearing, and gun shy, looked up from his place on a rug next to the garage service door. He didn't move. His limbs were frozen with age. Though Copper is his replacement, the new heir apparent, Sampson didn't rise to challenge the young pup.

I watched the sun climb over Lake Superior as I drove the back roads from Fredenberg to Two Harbors with a loose grip on the steering wheel and a travel mug of hot coffee in my right hand. Vapor rose from ditches lining the roadway. I pulled into the Two Harbors McDonald's drive-through and ordered an orange juice and an Egg McMuffin to go.

"Can he have a treat?" the clerk asked as she handed me a bag containing my breakfast.

"Sure," I answered.

The woman passed me two dog biscuits. I slipped them through a slit in the kennel.

"Thanks," I said before heading north on Highway 61.

When we arrived at the stream, Copper remained in his cage while I fished. I had no intention of letting a young Labrador disrupt the solitude of a morning spent in brook trout water.

My first cast of the day landed behind a small boulder. Water curled around stone, white and fast on its plunge towards the Big Lake. I felt a strike and set the hook. I reeled my line in. A brilliantly hued trout danced above the flowing stream. The fish arched and wheeled against the tension of the fishing line.

Splash.

The fish went free. Fog rolled off the river. Here and there, hints of autumn touched the maples, birch, and aspen lining the banks. Trout season was due to end on Monday. When I purchased my trout stamp and fishing license in May I vowed that I'd get in plenty of fishing. It's my first time out brook trout fishing this year.

A sleek doe, her nose wet, her eyes large and wary, stepped gingerly into the water. She entered the river twenty feet from where I stood. I watched the animal, its fur shiny in the fresh light, its caution evident. A yearling fawn nearly the size of its mother stepped into the river behind the doe. I stood transfixed, my dew worm floating off the bottom of the river. The animals stopped in the middle of the stream to drink.

"Hey," I shouted after allowing the deer an extended visit.

The animals were upwind. They did not smell my scent.

"Hello deer," I called out, waving my free arm like a maniac.

The doe's nostrils flared. Then, without so much as a broken twig, they were gone.

By noon I had four fat trout in the game pouch of my fishing vest. The sun was high. The brookies had disappeared beneath overhanging cedar roots and jumbled boulders to escape the warming day. By noon, I was hungry and convinced that the fish had stopped biting.

Lunch for the fisherman was a ham salad sandwich, a bottle of juice, a Hershey chocolate bar, and a bag of potato chips purchased from the Cooperative store in the little hamlet of Finland, Minnesota. Lunch for the retriever was an ample supply of dog kibble.

"Come on Cop," I called to the pup as I began to walk down an old logging road in search of ruffed grouse after finishing my sandwich on the tailgate of the van.

The dog lifted his head from the remnants of his meal before padding down the trail. He looked back at the dog kibble but didn't bolt for the food.

We walked the better part of two hours without seeing any game birds. Copper was perfect. He worked the edges of the trail with gusto. He never strayed more than a dozen paces ahead of me. He sniffed dead leaves and grass. He followed the scent of flickers and blue jays into the brush but always returned when called. After a bit, I raised Grandpa Jack's old .410, flicked the safety off, and pulled the trigger. I wasn't aiming at a bird. I discharged the shotgun to see the pup's

139

reaction. I wanted to be certain of Copper's abilities. Sampson, our old hound, despite a wonderful disposition, is so gun shy that he is totally useless in the field. I wanted to insure Copper didn't share the same sort of fear of loud noises.

Boom.

The pup was obviously without similar affliction. At the sound of the gun's discharge the young dog simply stopped and turned as if to ask:

"So did you hit the bird or what?"

"Good boy," I praised as I directed the pup into his kennel at the end of our walk. The dog's tail beat a steady pattern against the plastic walls of his cage. He let out a howl, the sort of lonesome call you'd associate with coon dogs. I emptied my shotgun and pulled my fishing gear out of the van.

For another hour, I worked a tiny rivulet in hopes of finding big trout. The section of the river I was on had yielded four or five nice trout the year before when I'd stumbled onto a beaver pond chock full of fish. But the water level in the creek was low and the streambed was littered with beaver leavings and silt. I worked hard to catch another brook trout but I was not rewarded for the effort.

Frozen Ground

There has been an absence of winter. Though the ground froze solid early this year, there is no snow cover.

Saturday. For the past several years, my two middle sons, Dylan and Christian, have been assigned the task of organizing our family's recycling. It's a job they're required to accomplish every month. Not that they easily comply with my requests to "take the recycling in". They don't. They're teenagers. It takes a lot of yelling and cajoling, accompanied by obvious threats, to compel their cooperation.

It's past ten o'clock in the morning. Both boys are fast asleep. I decide to accomplish two very dismal tasks on my own. One of them is to bring paper, plastic, glass, tin, and aluminum to the Recycling Center.

I dress for winter. The sun is shining. It's warm for December. Two or three days earlier in the week, the mercury reached forty-five degrees. I am hopeful that the warm spell will make my second task of the day manageable.

I begin my chores by dumping three barrels of assorted recyclables onto bare ground. Much of the refuse is contained in white trash bags. My first task is to open the bags and sort through the mess; plain glass in one pile; brown glass in another; tin cans to the side; aluminum into a cardboard box; plastic into a large black trash bag. Junk mail, newspapers, and magazines are deposited in plastic bins.

"Who in the world thinks this is acceptable?" I mutter aloud confronting a can of dog food with remnants of lamb and beef parts frozen to the container's interior wall.

There's no one around to hear, much less answer, my question. I find other examples of my family's malaise. Mayonnaise containers dotted with mold. Soup cans defiled by frozen chicken parts and solidified noodles.

"What's wrong?" René asks from the rear deck of our house. She's stepped outside into the warm December sunshine wearing her bathrobe.

"You people," I mumble.

"What are you talking about?" my wife asks defensively.

"Half this stuff can't be recycled," I remonstrate. "There's so much gunk stuck to the inside of these cans that the guy at the recycling shed will laugh at me if I try to give them to him."

"They're your sons," René observes.

Because I don't know who exactly left the bits and pieces of food in the various containers, I've include my spouse in my admonition, an implication which she ignores. Rather than continue the dialogue, I return to sorting through the mess.

Eventually, all of the items, including huge pieces of cardboard saved from the burning pile, portions of a box that housed Dylan's eighteenth birthday present (a new drafting table) make it into the rear of my old Lumina van. There is so much stuff packed into the Chevrolet that I have a hard time finding the shift lever to put the van into gear.

Thankfully, I've done a thorough job of sorting. I'm spared recriminations and haranguing at the recycling center. The old guy in charge is in a good mood and accepts all that my van carries. We have a nice chat about politics, as nice as can be expected given the present state of our democracy, before I head back home.

My second task of the day is more daunting. Sampson, our yellow Labrador retriever, passed away. I was in the Twin Cities at a judicial conference when he expired. Christian had been nursing the old codger along, feeding him special food, sneaking him into the house over the course of the dog's collapse.

The dog started to lose appreciable weight during the summer. René took him to the veterinarian. The vet x-rayed the rail thin old dog, took blood tests, but made no diagnosis. Our family suspicion was cancer of some sort. The vet suggested doing an ultrasound with the possibility of exploratory surgery. René and I vetoed putting the dog through any intrusive procedures. He was nearly fourteen, an old age for any dog, older still for an outdoor Labrador. There would be no more treatment, no more intervention. We both knew our decision meant that Sam wouldn't make it through the winter.

What we never contemplated was the reality of dealing with a dead family pet after the ground is frozen.

"Dylan, move the dog out to the storage shed," I had advised my second son over the phone from the judicial conference once I was apprised of the news.

"OK," he'd replied without emotion.

I approach the shed with trepidation. I don't know what to expect. Sam's been dead two weeks. It's taken that long for my schedule to clear so that I could deal with him. Or what used to be him. Despite the fact that I cherished his scraggly old face and white whiskers I haven't cried any tears for Sampson. I think it's because I've been grieving in bits and pieces throughout his steady decline. There's simply nothing left to cry about. He's been so sick for so long that the end was anticlimactic.

The dog's body is rigid and stiff and covered by an old quilt that Christian lovingly wrapped around him.

When I was eleven, growing up in Piedmont Heights in Duluth, I went out to feed my old black Labrador, Deuce, only to find the dog stone dead in his kennel. I know how hard losing a dog is to a boy. Chris tried to stave off the inevitable with love and a warm blanket. It simply wasn't enough.

I grab a shovel, a pick, and a sledge hammer hoping to loosen enough soil under the compost pile behind our shed so that I can properly bury the old dog. My efforts to dent the soil are rebuffed. I make no headway against the ground. I return the tools to the shed and stand over the dead animal.

"Need some help?"

My eldest son Matt appears behind me, his square shoulders framed by the shed's doorway.

"Grab one side of the blanket. We'll put him in the back of the van."

Though Sam is but a shadow of the dog he once was, he's still a load to carry. We struggle across frozen grass, the animal swaying between us on the quilt, as we advance towards the Lumina.

"Thanks," I say once we've placed Sam in the rear of the vehicle. I cover the dog with the blanket. Dignity, an attribute Sam displayed even in the depths of illness, remains important.

"What are you gonna do with him?"

I look away from my eldest son, a boy who has seen several dogs, innumerable cats, and two horses buried beneath the soil of our little place along the banks of the Cloquet River.

"I'll put him somewhere back in the woods on Grandpa's land."

"You sure? I don't think our other dogs will leave him alone."

I stare across the brown landscape.

"I'll cover him with trees and brush. I'll put him in the deep woods where they don't go."

Matt appears unconvinced. I open the driver's door, start the van, and head out. Matt's eyes follow the path of the Lumina as the vehicle descends the small hillock fronting our farmhouse. I know he thinks I should do more, that Sampson deserves a better end. It's all I can do to keep from crying as I drive away.

Bluefin Bay

We were invited to spend the weekend at Bluefin Bay Resort in Tofte, Minnesota, by our friends Jan and Bruce Larson. The winter was dismal in terms of opportunities to cross country ski. There was no snow. Not just a lack of snow but, literally, no snow in the woods around our home on the Cloquet River. In a normal winter, I'll ski the trails on our property several times a week for exercise. All told, from November until April of this year, I was only able to ski our trails twice. On both occasions, the snow cover was so meager that the bare ground scraped wax from the bottoms of my skis before I was halfway through my two-mile loop.

When the Larsons found out that they weren't going to be able to go with our "gang" of high school classmates on a planned Caribbean cruise (derisively dubbed *The Big Idea* by some of my friends) Jan called my wife René to invite us to share a weekend in Tofte. Jan had won the stay at the resort through a contest at work. The cost to us would be minimal. The economics of the invitation along with a promise of snow fit for skiing convinced us to accept Jan's offer.

"There are only two bedrooms and a bathroom," Jan notes as we arrive in the second story condominium unit. "I pictured it to have a living room," she adds as Bruce deposits luggage on the floor of one of the bedrooms.

I poke my head around the corner and smile.

"We can all get cozy in our jammies and watch TV in your room."

"I don't want to see you in your jammies," Bruce moans.

I check out our bedroom. René is already busy unpacking her suitcase. We're staying two nights. She brought enough clothing for a month.

"Why'd you pack all that stuff?" I ask.

"Never can have too many choices," my bride responds.

145

I explore the space and discover a ladder leading to a small loft area overlooking our bedroom.

"Cool", I say as I climb the ladder.

The height of the ceiling precludes me from standing. There's a skylight above my head. The floor of the loft is carpeted.

The perfect place to read, I think, realizing that my wife won't be too happy if I spend significant time engrossed in the novel I brought with me.

It's Friday night. We're staying until Sunday. Whether we ski both Saturday and Sunday depends upon the weather. The four of us pile into René's Toyota RAV before dinner and drive to the resort's outdoor hot tub. The temperature has plummeted. It's below zero. There's no moon. Small shards of starlight interrupt the black sky as Bruce and I remove the canvas cover of the hot tub and climb in. Vapor hangs over the simmering water. Our wives join us. Wine is poured. No one disturbs us. After a long soak, we return to our rooms, dress, and wander over to the resort's restaurant. After a wonderful meal we head back to the condo for wine and contests. Boys against the Girls. *Trivial Pursuit*. The boys kick butt. It's a perfect evening.

The next morning we eat big breakfasts, drink pots of hot coffee, and talk about our kids at a table overlooking Lake Superior. The window glass is frosted. Waves crash against the rocky shoreline and an old concrete pier extends into gray water. The mercury hasn't climbed. It's hovering at five below. The sky is open and displays a surreal blue canopy devoid of clouds.

We drive away from the Lake, climbing a high ridge to the west in the Larson's Ford Escape. Four sets of skis and poles rattle in the cargo area of the Ford. The roadway leads us from the shoreline of Lake Superior into the hardwood forests of the Sawtooth Mountains. I study a map of ski trails that the resort provides its guests. Bruce finds the parking lot for the trail we want to ski and parks the Ford.

A father and two children move ponderously. We watch them struggle up a steep hill. The trail they are following is poorly defined. Aspen and alders interrupt the path. We clip our ski bindings into place and follow the kids. The family comes to rest at the top of the slope. We pass by. The track narrows. The woods thicken. We find ourselves encircled by trees.

"I don't think this is a state ski trail," René laments as we move through ankle deep powder.

It really doesn't matter to me whether we're lost or not. We've found enough snow to ski and ski smoothly, something that has been impossible to do all winter. I've missed the glide of cross-country skis against snow. I've missed the feeling of crisp below-zero air on my bare skin.

"Maybe it just doesn't get used much," I offer.

"I dunno," Bruce adds, "I think René's on to something."

We continue on. The forest opens up ahead of us. We've found the trail that we were supposed to be on.

"Here we are," I say proudly, as if my wilderness skills have saved us. "I told you we'd find the trail."

My companions look at me but say nothing. I know what my wife is thinking. She's mulling over the myriad of times I've misread roadmaps on family trips leading us off our intended path. René must be in a very good mood. She doesn't remind me of those occasions.

My ski trail at home has a small stand of sugar maples at the top of what I call the Ridge Trail. Here, along a ridge parallel to Lake Superior, we ski through acre after acre of magnificent mature maple forest. The undergrowth is nearly nonexistent. The openness of this hardwood forest is in stark contrast to the tight woodlands that border my property.

I pass a beaver lodge protruding defiantly above pond ice. At the intersection of two trails, Bruce and I stop to wait for our wives. Two deer bound in front of René. Her head is lowered. Her concentration is fixed. She doesn't see the animals.

The snow cover peters out before we reach Highway 61. I cringe as the bottoms of my new skis traverse rocks and gravel. I give in and carry my skis the final few yards to the end of the trail.

Later that afternoon, the four of us soak in the outside spa. The sky remains clear. The air remains cold. A stiff breeze rustles the hot water of the spa. My hair freezes solid. A gorgeous young black woman joins us. A robust white male, his skin artificially tanned, enters the tub holding what looks to be a tumbler of scotch. He sits next to the woman. We learn that he's a professional photographer and that she's a professional model. They're in Tofte to shoot a cosmetics commercial. It appears from the man's diction and mannerisms that he's gay.

What safer way to send a beautiful model out into the world than to entrust her to a companion who's totally disinterested in her, I think.

The photographer takes a shine to Bruce, a point I'll likely use from time and time over the years when and if it's necessary. I theorize the man is attracted to Bruce's naturally curly hair. What else could it be?

Dinner at the historic Lutsen Lodge located on Highway 61 north of Tofte is wonderful. We laugh and reminisce, telling stories that we've all heard countless times before. Retelling old pearls of history is something good friends tolerate.

Back at the condo, we resume playing *Trivial Pursuit*. This time, the girls win the first game. There's an upset in the making. I put down my wine glass and concentrate on the contest. Bruce and I pull out the second game. We also win the third game, and with it, the match, by the narrowest of margins. Both teams had gathered all their "pies" but we are able to answer a question selected by the girls. Victory is ours. The natural order of things is restored. I can drive home tomorrow satisfied.

In Search of Snow

"South Dakota?" the female attorney queried. "I've never heard of anyone going to South Dakota to downhill ski."

I was sitting behind my bench in the Duluth Courthouse. I'd just finished a hearing and was shooting the breeze with the attorneys after the defendant and police officers had left.

"Terry Peak," I explained. "It's in the Black Hills, about twelve hours from here. I wanted to find a place that was challenging but close. It's over a thousand vertical, making it steeper than anything around here."

The woman's skeptical look didn't abate.

"South Dakota?" my wife René posited as I explained my plan to her later that same evening, "who goes to South Dakota to downhill ski?"

I bit my lip.

"Well, I'm only going if they have snow. Right now their website shows that the hill is half open."

Our conversation took place in early January. At the time the ground around our home in the country was devoid of snow. Minnesota wasn't alone. Most of the Northern United States, with the exception of New England and Up-State New York, remained barren of snow cover. Even Upper Peninsula Michigan, where residents normally tunnel their way from their front door to the street through drifts, lacked significant snow.

"I read about Terry Peak when I was a kid. It always looked like a nice place to try," I offered.

"Have a good time by yourself," René replied. "I can't afford to take a week off from work. I need the time off in March when we go on our cruise."

We were planning to celebrate our twenty-fifth wedding anniversary in the Caribbean with seven other couples from high school. We were set to leave March first. In early January, while my long suffering spouse was looking

149

forward to sun, beaches, and down time away from our four sons, I was thinking snow.

"If you go it'll be hard to get Jack to daycare by eight in the morning if I need to be at work in Biwabik by eight-thirty," she reminded me.

I stared at my corn flakes. I was sitting at the dining room table surrounded by another gray Minnesota winter day. It seemed like the sun hadn't presented itself for a lifetime. The trace snow covering the grass in our backyard was a reminder that my cross-country skis were accumulating dust in the garage. There was not enough snow to consider touring our property on my primitive trails. In truth, there was not enough snow to make a snowball.

"I'll take Jack and Chris with me," I said.

"Have a good time," my wife repeated, cognizant that driving twelve hours in a van across Southern Minnesota and the entire State of South Dakota with quarreling siblings, ages five and fifteen, would be a true test of my patience.

I kept track of the snowfall in the Black Hills via www.terrypeak.com, the ski hill's website. Two weeks before our slated, departure after convincing Christian, my fifteen year old son that the trip, even without significant snow, would be an adventure (and a week off of school), I remained unconvinced that there would be enough snow in the Black Hills to make the journey worthwhile. I began planning alternative skiing scenarios: an overnight trip to Lutsen; a couple of days in Upper Peninsula Michigan. I made the mistake of sharing these possibilities with my teenaged son.

"I don't want to go to Lutsen," Chris lamented. "You said we were going to South Dakota."

I'd already made a reservation for a hotel room at the Deadwood Holiday Inn Express. Deadwood, a historic venue turned gambling destination by the South Dakota State Legislature to insure a steady stream of revenue for the old mining town, is only five miles from Terry Peak. The price for a room in Deadwood was right- thirty-five bucks a night, breakfast included. Five nights for two hundred dollars. One night's lodging at Lutsen would cost as much or more than our entire trip.

Snow began to fall in the Black Hills during the third week in January. I watched the white powder accumulate daily via the Internet. Runs opened. Lifts began operating. By the last week of the month nearly all of the slopes were ready for use, but doubters persisted.

"I thought you were headed out West," an attorney commented at a dinner party the Saturday evening before we left for South Dakota.

"I thought you were going as soon as the trial ended," a female lawyer added referencing a murder case that had taken up an entire month of my judicial career.

There had been a danger that the jury, which had concluded its deliberations the day before, would need more time to decide the case, postponing our trip.

"Tomorrow," I replied. "My two youngest sons and I leave tomorrow."

"Montana or Colorado?" the first attorney asked.

"South Dakota," I responded.

I watched shrouds of doubt color the lawyers' faces. Their reactions caused my stomach to rumble. An unpleasant premonition presented itself.

"I didn't know you could downhill ski in South Dakota," the woman replied.

Sunday morning. This is to be the last road trip for our tired 1995 Lumina van. I read the odometer as we pull onto I-35 in Midway Township south of Duluth. The vehicle has 210,000 miles on it. I'm hoping to squeeze at least 1,700 more miles out of the engine.

Chris sits in the passenger seat. His attention is riveted on a book. Jack is sitting behind Chris, his imagination occupied by several Star Wars figurines. I've removed two rear seats to accommodate our ski gear and luggage.

"How many hours to Rapid City?" Chris asks never removing his eyes from his book.

"Twelve."

The teenager nods his head. Sounds of clashing light sabers erupt from the rear seat as the old van accelerates

151

towards the promise of snow.

"The big building on the hillside is Gustavus."

I point out Gustavus Adolphus College to my fifteen year old son Chris as we slowly cruise the main street of St. Peter, Minnesota.

"Why aren't there any trees?" the teen asks.

"A tornado wiped them out."

The Lumina heads south on US 169. Around LeSuer, home of the Jolly Green Giant, we began to follow the Minnesota River Valley. The waterway's flood plain is fringed with oaks, cottonwoods, and low ridges. A light drizzle is falling. There is no snow. The Minnesota River is frozen but only hesitantly so.

We follow Minnesota Highway 60 as it slices through the farms of Southwestern Minnesota. The rain intensifies. To a native Minnesotan, encountering rain in early February, in any part of the state, is unnerving. The exposed black earth of the region is moist from rainfall. There are no snow banks, no drifts, not the slightest indication that it is winter. We pass lakes covered with meager ice, fisherman poised gingerly over their holes in the mist, their trucks brazenly parked on the suspect surfaces of lakes. These ponds are prairie potholes sculpted by glaciers, the same glaciers that removed the rich top soil from Canada and deposited it here to the eternal benefit of Minnesota farmers.

Even in small town America, one cannot escape the Golden Arches. I pull the beleaguered Lumina into a McDonald's in Windom, Minnesota for lunch. As we eat, I read a local tourist handout and discover all the reasons why one should visit, perhaps even move, to this small town on the cusp of Iowa. Downhill skiing, the purpose for our trip, is not mentioned as an endearing attribute of Windom, Minnesota.

Near Worthington we connect with I-90. It begins to rain in earnest. We enter Rock County, the southwestern-most county in Minnesota, the only county in the state without a natural lake.

"Are you sure there's snow out in the Black Hills?" Chris asks as he looks up from reading a book about The Simpsons.

My teenager is a compulsive watcher of the neo-classic cartoon. His room is filled with images of Homer, Lisa, Bart, Maggie, and Marge.

"The website said Terry Peak has plenty of snow," I reply.

"I hope so," the kid grumbles.

We pass through Sioux Falls, South Dakota. The sky remains gray. The van's windshield wipers contend with light rain. Mitchell, South Dakota, renowned departure point for pheasant hunters, retreats in the rearview mirror. Night falls. Traffic speeds west at a comfortable seventy five miles per hour. As the landscape descends into the valley of the Missouri River at Chamberlain, visibility disappears. The rain changes to thick sludge. A dangerous mixture of snow and sleet cloaks the freeway. The night is so black it leaves the impression that we are entering a deep forest. It's an illusion. There are no trees out here on the prairie: only rolling hills giving way to incessant plains.

"I'm gonna slow down," I lament, the front end of the van feeling less than secure as we round corners. "I don't think we're gonna make it to Deadwood in twelve hours."

Jack is snoring loudly in the back seat. Chris is staring at the inky shroud enveloping our vehicle. Big flakes of white plaster the van's windshield. The snow intermingles with clean rain. The van's wipers thrash wildly at the mixture.

By the time we reach Wall, site of the famous drugstore, I'm wringing wet from nervous sweat. My hands are sore from clenching the steering wheel. The roadway is a nightmare. Traffic is reduced to crawling along at twenty-five miles per hour. Truckers stop and put out flares, blocking the inside lane in its entirety while they put chains on the tires of their rigs.

"This is a lot of fun," I moan as I pull off to refuel. A local sheriff and a South Dakota State Trooper are chatting with the cashier in the truck stop as I approach to pay for my gas.

153

"I slid right through the stop sign on No. 14," the deputy admits. "Locked 'er up and slid right on through."

"It's plenty nasty out there, that's for sure," the trooper agrees.

"This is the first snow we've seen since Northern Minnesota," I add.

"Where you from?" the deputy asks.

"Duluth."

"Long ways from home," the officer says through a smile.

"Headed towards Deadwood, to ski," I say, returning my wallet to my pocket.

The officers refrain from further comment. I exit the station and confront a brisk wind. The weather doesn't let up until we are on the outskirts of Rapid City. It's nearly nine-thirty Mountain Time, ten-thirty Central time.

"What do ya think?" I ask Christian. "Should we stay overnight in Rapid City and try to make Deadwood tomorrow morning?"

"How far is it to the hotel in Deadwood?"

"I gotta go potty," Jack interrupts.

"In a minute, Jack," I admonish. "It's thirty miles to Deadwood," I advise.

"Let's go for it," Chris decides. "I want to get to our hotel."

"OK."

We make a pit stop so Jack can do his business. When we reconnect with I-90, we find our path to the Black Hills blocked by two state patrol cars. The freeway north is closed due to the sleet.

"What do we do now?" Chris asks.

"Is there another way, a back way, to Deadwood from here?" I ask.

Chris studies a travel atlas.

"We can take 385 west, then north and come in the back way through Lead," he advises.

The drive through the canyon is harrowing. The road twists and turns behind the beginnings of the Black Hills.

Black spruce and lodge pole pine-covered ridges soar above us. We pass few homes.

"Look at all the snow."

The reports from Terry Peak have not been exaggerated. The roadway is lined with high banks of plowed powder.

"This road's under construction," I observe as we crawl through the storm. "There's no more pavement."

Huge mounds of snow-covered earth line the highway. The Lumina's tires spin on loose gravel. The climb seems endless.

And then, we are in Lead. The bright lights of the high school, the Burger King, and assorted other businesses greet us. We are five minutes from our hotel. It's ten-thirty, three hours past our anticipated arrival. As we check in at the Holiday Inn Express in Deadwood, the clerk smiles.

"Your wife's on the phone. She's worried about you."

I take the phone from the young woman.

"René?" I ask.

"You OK?"

"It was hell on the freeway," I admit. "I'll tell you about it once we check in. I'll call you right back."

My kids sit on suitcases while I fill out paperwork. Tomorrow, we're going to find out if the trip to Terry Peak was worth the drive.

Morning comes. I roust Christian and Jack, from bed. I've slept fitfully. Jack and I shared a Queen-sized bed. My rest was disturbed because Jack has a tendency to spin around like a top when he sleeps, which means his feet usually end up kicking me in the small of my back. Last night was no exception. I felt tiny toes prodding my spine on a number of occasions.

The hotel offers a nice continental breakfast. After we've cleaned up, we amble down to the lobby to eat. I eavesdrop as ranchers and other folks involved with livestock wander in and out of the dining area. The Rapid City newspaper I picked up at the front desk indicates there's a stock show in town. The local television news playing on a big

155

screen in the lobby recounts the antics of little kids, boys and girls no bigger than Jack, attempting to ride bucking sheep as part of the stock event. Twelve hours from home, my sons and I are immersed in the American West, standing out in our downhill ski clothing amongst Stetsons and finely polished cowboy boots like proverbial sore thumbs.

"This sure is a long way up," Chris says as our van chugs through the winding terrain of the Black Hills.

We pass back through the town of Lead on our way to the Terry Peak ski area. Conifers lining the steep hills on either side of the two-lane highway are coated with thick snow. The sky is empty, high, and blue. I turn at the "Terry Peak" sign.

"That's the way to Deer Mountain," I say, pointing to a sign for another local downhill ski area. "Maybe we'll spend our third day there."

Jack remains quiet. He's dressed in a black ski jacket, black snow pants, black mittens, Sorels, ski helmet, liner, and goggles. I can't see his eyes because of the tinted lenses of the goggles but I know from the inclination of his head that he's awake and considering his surroundings.

Chris maintains silence. He appears to be sleeping or perhaps unconsciously pondering whether or not this trip, a journey of fifteen hours due to the storm we passed through on the way here, was worth the effort.

"There's the hill," I say as the road makes a sudden pitch upward.

Off to our left two high-speed chair lifts climb from the base of the ridge to the ski area's summit. The top of Terry Peak is essentially bare, topped by a cluster of radio antennas and little else. At 7, 100 feet the hill is significant. With over 1,100 feet of vertical it should be challenging.

"Shouldn't we turn?" Chris asks as we pass the Nevada Gulch parking lot.

"We're going to the beginner area so I can work with Jack," I relate. "You can get to this part of the hill from there."

"OK."

We park in front of the main chalet. The three of us put on our ski boots in the car before entering the building. I approach the only clerk at the ticket desk and hand her my credit card. The price is $35.00 for a full day for Chris and me. Jack's free. Spirit Mountain, back in our hometown of Duluth, Minnesota charges $35.00 for a half-day ticket. Given that Terry Peak boasts more vertical, $35.00 for a full day ticket is a bargain.

Outside I help Jack step into his bindings. Because I'm teaching Jack, we don't need ski poles. A tether secures Jack to my body. The connection will allow me to control his speed and teach him the finer points of the snowplow. You can buy special equipment for this purpose. I use a lunge line left over from when we owned horses. Jack doesn't know the difference and it works essentially the same. I used the same system to teach Chris. Before the lunge line, I used an old lead rope, again, from our horse barn, to teach Dylan, my second son, how to ski.

I taught my eldest son Matt to ski by skiing with him between my legs. I also used this technique with my brother Dave and my sister Annie. Skiing with a kid between your legs isn't easy. It does a number on your knees and lower back. The tether is a vast improvement.

"By the end of this trip," I say to my youngest son, "you'll be skiing without my help."

Jack smiles. Chris remains silent. I sense the teenager doubts my prognostication.

The beginner's chairlift floats along steel cable through cool air. Jack, Chris, and I glide through early morning light surrounded by snow-covered pines and spruce reminiscent of iced Christmas cookies.

"Why don't you check out the harder runs?" I suggest to Chris when we reach the top of the beginner hill.

The teenager nods and slides towards Surprise, an easier run leading to one of the high-speed chairlifts. I watch Christian make graceful turns until the slope of the hill ends my view.

I loop the tether around Jack, secure the end of the line in my right glove, and urge him to move forward. His little skis pick up speed. My son makes no attempt to slow his descent or to turn as he roars down the hill.

"Put the fronts of your skis in a "v", like this," I demonstrate at the bottom of the slope. "That way you can turn and stop."

Jack merely smiles. On our next run, he resumes his quest to see how fast and how straight he can ski.

Towards the end of our first day, I convince Chris to watch Jack while I ski without a thirty pound child attached to my wrist. I begin these private excursions on the "blue" or "more difficult" runs. Kussy, the main hill running next to the Kussy Express lift, is a gem. Though listed as "more difficult" (as opposed to "black diamond" or "most difficult"), when I ski Kussy from top to bottom without stopping, my knees shake. That, in my view, is the mark of a real ski hill. After making a couple of runs on Kussy, Homestake, and Empress, I tackle the black diamonds. Holy Terror, Ben Hur, and lower Kussy all challenge my forty-eight year old knees and hips. I bounce. I twist. I turn, remaining upright. Finding a steady cadence to my descent, I have a whale of a good time. I remember why I love to ski.

"Forty-five minutes," Chris moaned at the end of the day as I encounter my sons at the bottom of the beginner hill. "You said you were going to take two runs."

I smile.

"I lied."

"Jack and I fell asleep on the benches in the chalet," Chris asserts. His dander is still up.

"Let's go back to the hotel for a swim."

Light powder snow greets us when we arrive at Terry Peak the next morning. It's 9:00am. The hill is just coming to life. There are few skiers. A solid wall of clouds envelopes the summit. The antenna towers and guy wires disappear in gray. Our view of the surrounding peaks and valleys is obliterated. Standing at the top of Kussy with Jack once again safely controlled by the tether, I watch Chris plummet towards the base of the slope. A temporary lapse in the squall reveals blue sky. A hint of the sun's disk appears. The resulting view recalls another ski trip with my wife René, in years past, to the Green Mountains, though the spruce trees, which give the

Black Hills their distinctive coloration cannot be mistaken for the maples of Killington, Vermont.

Jack learns. By the end of our second day of skiing, he makes three consecutive runs down the beginner slope without a spill and without the aid of the tether.

"Wanna try Deer Mountain tomorrow?" I ask Chris. We're sitting on the edge of a precipice in the Lumina. Chris is videotaping the main face of Terry Peak through the open window of the van as we head back to Deadwood.

"Sure," he says, his attention riveted on the display screen of the camera.

"Sounds good," I agree.

"I wanna go swimming," Jack laments, his head leaning heavily, the effort of two days of downhill skiing enticing him towards a nap.

"Pizza first," I say.

A whining noise makes its presence known from the rear seat. I put the vehicle in gear. The Chevrolet creeps forward.   Contented snoring replaces my youngest son's objection to dinner. My eyes follow the blacktop as the vehicle negotiates the curving roadway into Lead, South Dakota. I am mindful that, uncharacteristically, one of my wild notions actually paid off.

Snow falls. Thick flakes drift through the silver sky adding a layer of fluff to sixteen inches of new snow already on the ground. My sons are bundled up in their ski clothing as our van pulls up to the base of Deer Mountain Ski Area.

We spent the past two days skiing Terry Peak, the best-known ski hill in the area. Until I saw the "Deer Mountain" sign along the highway just beyond the Terry Peak turn-off, I didn't even know there was another downhill ski area in South Dakota. I convinced Chris that we should spend our last day skiing at Deer Mountain. Jack wasn't consulted. He's pretty much just along for the ride.

"There's no one here," Chris says as I turn off the vehicle's engine.

A moderate slope rises above us as we exit the vehicle. Unlike Terry Peak, which has the attributes of a subtle mountain, Deer Mountain is reminiscent of ski areas in Minnesota, Wisconsin, and Upper Michigan: More a hill than peak.

"Looks OK to me," I reply.

After pulling on our ski boots and toting our poles and skis to the front of the chalet, we enter the building to purchase lift tickets. Inside, other than a smattering of employees, the only other people in the chalet are several dozen enthusiastic young Native American boys and girls under the apparent supervision of five or six middle school teachers. It's clear the kids are here not to ski but to slide on Deer Mountain's inner tube hill.

I approach a counter and pay for our lift tickets. Once again the prices are reasonable. Jack skis free. Chris's ticket is $24.00. Mine is $27.00. I grab a trail map and study it. The diagram shows two hills connected by a tunnel. I'm encouraged that the area boasts more runs, though less vertical drop, than Terry Peak.

"Let's go," I urge the boys as I rise from a picnic table and head towards the door.

The four-person chair lift is amazingly slow. Instead of being whisked through the swirling white, past majestic lodge pole pines to the snow-enveloped top of the hill, we dally through the air at an agonizing pace.

By the time we arrive at the summit, the falling snow has completely eliminated our view. Still, there's a compensatory magnificence about the slow parade of the snowfall.

"Chris, lead us on," I urge.

I wrap a tether line around Jack's waist. Despite the fact that Jack negotiated the beginner's slope without the safety rope by the end of our second day at Terry Peak, Deer Mountain doesn't offer a hill modest enough for Jack to ski without the tether.

"Here goes," Chris shouts, pushing off with his poles.

We ski an open bowl. There's a trail off the top of the bowl to the tunnel but its closed, effectively eliminating a good portion of Deer Mountain from use.

"Snow plow," I command as my youngest son and I curl over the cusp of the ridge and fall into the natural hollow.

The snow is thigh deep and fluffy. Jack weaves and bobs like a prizefighter but does little to slow his speed. I dig the edges of my skis into the base of the snow pack to slow us down. The kid wants to go fast.

"Slow down," I admonish. Jack doesn't acknowledge my existence.

I yank hard on the tether spilling the kid to the ground. Standing over him I emphasize that I'm the teacher and that he's the pupil.

"Every time you don't listen, I'll pull the rope and you'll sit on your butt. Understand?"

Jack looks up. I can't see his eyes because of his goggles but I know he's considering his options. It's an open question whether he'll acquiesce to my demands. He nods slightly. I nod back. The crisis passes.

After a quick lunch of room-temperature leftover Pizza Hut pizza and cold soda, I leave Chris in charge of Jack. I intend to take a couple of runs by myself. Exiting the warm building, I note that there are less than twenty patrons taking advantage of the beautiful snowfall. It's Wednesday, the first day of the week that Deer Mountain is open. The locals are probably working. Even so, you'd expect a few die-hard skiers from Rapid City, only a half hour away, to play hooky on a day like today.

My ski poles are missing. Actually, they're my wife René's poles. I'm using hers because they're in better shape than mine are. I search the perimeter of the chalet on the off chance that someone picked them up by mistake and set them down in a different spot. I don't find my wife's poles.

"Someone took my ski poles," I explain to a young woman at the ticket desk.

"I'll tell the lift operators to watch for them," she says after taking down a description of the stolen items.

"Seems odd anyone would take them today," I offer. "There's no one here."

Even with Chris's help the poles are never found.

161

"I need to rent poles," I advise a kid in charge of rentals in the basement of the chalet. "Mine were stolen."

"Help yourself," the young man says. "We don't charge for poles."

"Thanks," I reply, wondering how a ski area with so few customers can afford to be so generous. I also wonder how I'm going to explain to my wife that she's now without downhill ski poles.

I hit the black diamonds and soon discover that, while the top half of the runs, the portions gentle enough for grooming equipment, are fantastic, the middle portions, which are too steep to groom, are an ugly mix of powder and frozen ruts. You don't know where the ruts are because of the fresh snow. Despite the deception I take four or five runs on the toughest hills. I manage to keep my nose out of the snow, but just barely.

I ski with Jack for the remainder of the afternoon. Chris seems content to discover the runs of Deer Mountain on his own. By four o'clock I've had enough. Three days of skiing with a five-year-old have made my calves tight and my lower back sore. We leave Deer Mountain without René's ski poles.

The ride home through South Dakota is uneventful. Though it's only a few degrees above zero and the wind is whipping across the plains, the roads are clear and the sun is out. Just before Sioux Falls I swing north, take the freeway twenty miles or so up the road towards Brookings, and then head east again on a two lane towards Pipestone, Minnesota.

Music blares from the CD player. The Lumina, pushing 212,000 miles, races home. In Pipestone, we connect with Minnesota 23 and turn north. We skirt a metallic forest of windmills erected on the cold and desolate plateau of southeastern Minnesota. The blades of the giant pinwheels spin slowly, creating a lazy elevated ballet.

Near Pipestone we encounter the first evidence of winter we've seen since leaving Rapid City. A regional storm apparently pushed through the Minnesota River Valley surrounding Granite Falls, depositing ten to twelve inches of fresh snow on previously naked earth.

James McMurtry
Iris Dement
Neil Young
Brenda Weiler
The Grateful Dead
Leslie West and Mountain
Bruce Springsteen
Arlo Guthrie
Crosby, Stills, Nash, and Young.
Lynn Miles

I force my kids to listen to my music until night blankets the Minnesota countryside.

"Put on Pink Floyd," I urge Chris.

We pass the Black Bear Casino in Carlton as I make my request.

"Who's 'Pink Floyd'"? my son asks.

I sing a line or two from "Money", one of the most famous songs on the record.

"OK, OK, stop with the singing already. I'll put it on," Chris moans.

Jack is asleep in the back seat. Green dashboard lights taunt my tired eyes. Twelve hours of driving. Only a few more miles to go. There's not a star, much less the moon, visible in the sky. The first track on the album begins:

Breathe, breathe in the air...

It's been a perfect trip.

Another Hunting Story

Autumn has arrived. The first traces of snow litter the ground in stark contrast to the yellow stubble left after haying. I'm sitting in my Honda Passport SUV in the driveway outside my house, waiting for Jack, my six year old son, and Christian, Jack's sixteen year old brother.

The vehicle idles smoothly. The radio is off. The sun breaches the tree line. It's a lovely October day. As I sit waiting to drive my two youngest sons to school, a large cottontail dashes across the short grass bordering the blacktop drive. The rabbit's run is crazed: A zigging and zagging that has no obvious purpose behind it, at least not until I see the kestrel.

Over the past several years, a family of kestrels has taken up residence on our land. From time to time, adult birds of this diminutive branch of the hawk family sit on Jack's swing set contemplating the pasture surrounding our house, waiting for an errant mouse or mole to show itself. These birds of prey are smaller than a robin. A field mouse is a banquet for a kestrel. I watch in amazement as the frantic bird dips and flits above the rabbit, the bird obviously bent on somehow overpowering the far larger mammal.

The rabbit has every opportunity to simply disappear. Tangled weeds, shrubs, and scrub afford an easy retreat for the hare but the rabbit doesn't bolt for the woods. Instead, the hare sprints along the edge of our field tantalizing the overmatched hawk into attack after futile attack. Unlike other times I've witnessed similar encounters, usually between red tail hawks and cottontails, during which the frightened rabbit usually succumbs due to sheer terror, the cottontail doesn't appear the least bit concerned about its fate.

The dance continues for a few minutes. The kestrel finally gives up. The rabbit skitters into the undergrowth. The boys climb into the car for the ride to school.

Christian has expressed an interest in hunting. After completing a gun safety course, I allowed him to use my grandfather's old Stevens Savage .410 side-by-side to hunt partridge and rabbits on our property. I'm not there to witness it but on one of his very first excursions into the woods with a shotgun and our year and a half old Labrador, Copper, Chris nailed a partridge in mid-flight. The dog, after rousting the partridge from its hiding place apparently retrieved the downed bird despite having never carried anything in its mouth beyond the commonplace ball or stick. It's a story I'm certain deserves a more detailed telling than I've given it here. It's a tale for Christian to write.

Today is Sunday. Chris and I are exploring the backwoods near Wolf Lake in rural St. Louis County. Copper sleeps in the back of the Passport while I drive down a gravel road and read a map at the same time.

"Papoose Lake should be around here somewhere," I say, my eyes darting from page to windshield to prevent disaster. "There must be a trail somewhere off to the left."

A sign next to the road we're on indicates that the bridge that once spanned the Cloquet River up ahead no longer exists. The road apparently ends at the River. I drive until we find high ground. The forest looks grousy. I park the car.

"This is as good a place as any," I say. "Load up the shotgun and let Copper go to work."

We walk a narrow trail parallel to the river. On a bank overlooking the Cloquet, I'm treated to a surprise.

"Chris," I call out. My son and the dog are off in the distance in pursuit of birds.

"Ya."

"This is that sand bank where we saw the wood turtles. Remember, when we canoed down from Indian Lake?"

The knoll I'm standing on pitches sharply into the River. Indeed, it is the spot where we stopped our canoe to photograph rare and elusive wood turtles found only along this stretch of the Cloquet.

Chris walks up, stands besides me, nods, and then returns to the hunt.

We enter what once was a pasture. Insistent jack pine interrupt the dormant hay field. The trees appear intent upon returning forest to an open space created a century ago by man's incessant need to harvest timber.

"This will work," I say as I walk behind the dog and my son.

Earlier in the trip, I had pulled the Passport into a boat launch on Wolf Lake in hope that viewing the lakeshore would be useful in visualizing the landscape depicted in my latest novel. The vacant field we traverse supplies similar vindication. The waving grass and the decaying pine stumps fit the feel and emotion of the story I am writing, the story of Finnish immigration to Northeastern Minnesota.

I'm searching for Papoose Lake so I can experience the shoreline of that insignificant pond, to smell the air, to listen to the wind rustling the vegetation surrounding the lake. I intend to include a Finnish homestead on the shores of Papoose Lake in my story. Though fiction doesn't require perfection, it does require at least some level of honesty. One doesn't try to insert a lake where no lake could possibly exist. But one can take a vacant pasture and, using the time-traveling abilities of pen and paper, place a turn-of-the-century Finnish homestead on that field.

"This could be the farm in my story," I say, thinking aloud.

Chris pays me no mind. He follows the quickening stride of the retriever into a thick grove of jack pines. Two ruffed grouse burst from cover and flee to the other side of the river. No shots are fired.

We see no other birds. Chris and the dog hunt intently for two more hours. The sky begins to darken. We pack up and head for home. Along the highway, we pass deer nibbling grass located next to the pavement. We count over forty deer in the span between the hamlet of Brimson and Island Lake. Only one of the animals has antlers.

I park the Honda in our garage and let Copper out the back hatch. Chris unfolds his legs and exits the car with cased shotgun in hand. Though my third son didn't shoot a

166

partridge, I was able to give some order to narrative and snippets of dialogue that had been crowding my mind. From that perspective it was a very productive hunt.

The Biggest Striker

It's not often that you get to share a tall tale about the game of soccer. The sport is so, shall we say, refined. Sure, soccer has a slim margin of mythology to it. But the sport's mystique, at least here in America, isn't on par with ice hockey, American football, or baseball. Tall tales just don't abound in the soccer world. Pelé pointing down the field and calling a goal during the World Cup? Nope. Mia Hamm getting turned around and scoring on her own goaltender? Never happened. A father well over fifty years old coming back from retirement after a legendary career to play middle fielder with his sons? Impossible. But there is at least one true story that will forever be etched in Hermantown youth soccer lore. This is that story.

The U-16 Boys' Hermantown Havoc Traveling Team takes the field, their white and black jerseys billowing in a warm summer breeze. A team from Blaine, a Twin Cities suburb, warms up at the north end of the field. Balls sail through the air. Goalies leap to snatch leather spheres out of the atmosphere or swat them to the ground with vengeance. The sun settles in the west over the rooftops of the Hermantown Community Church and its more liberal counterpart, Trinity Episcopal Church. Heavy commuter traffic zooms past the soccer complex. The parking lot at the Community Church is empty. There is a scarcity of movement across Maple Grove at the Deerfield Apartments. The air cools as the sun descends.

I'm sitting on a canvas camping chair. The wind switches, comes from the east, from the Big Lake, making it even colder. Goose bumps form on my skin. I wrap myself in a blue Hawks blanket. I keep an eye on Jack as he plays with another little boy on a gym set a good hundred feet or so away.

The game begins. I watch my son Christian, a middle fielder, a kid that I used to coach, miss an easy steal. He chases after a Blaine player advancing up the near sidelines. The west side of the field is lined with blankets and portable chairs like the one I'm using. Fans supporting their teams separate into camps: a necessity so that fistfights don't break out over insensitive comments or observations. The empty space between the parents, a soccer-No-Man's-Land, is crucial to preserving peace.

I hear my eldest son Matt bellowing at his players. Matt stands across the field beneath a portable awning sheltering the reserve players for the Havoc. His arms are crossed. His voice is clear and direct.

"Use your support," he yells to his players. "Short passes," he urges.

Chris moves the ball past a Blaine forward. Free of pressure he studies the field and launches a looping pass to Jake Sedor, one of the forwards, who is racing down the right sidelines towards the opposing goal. As I focus on Jake's run, a large black object appears in my peripheral field of vision across Maple Grove Road.

"Oh my Lord," I exclaim as my brain recognizes the intruding mass. "It's a big bull moose."

Sure enough, a lanky, slender shouldered male moose canters his way across the blacktop road between passing vehicles. The animal resembles a very ugly and overly tall draft horse. I watch the animal saunter onto a vacant soccer field next to where the boys are playing their game. The contest stops. No whistle is blown. The players are simply awestruck by the sight of a bull moose standing on mown grass. Play is suspended by silent accord.

"Wow," says a mother of one of the Blaine players. "I've never seen a moose before."

My bet is that most of the folks standing at the Stebner complex this day have never seen a moose. And even if they have, they've never seen one completely exposed; unprotected by swamp, trees, or other natural vegetation. I know I haven't. Not in all the canoe trips I've taken or in all the hours I've spent hunting. I've seen my share of the largest member of the deer family. But not like this. Not with an evangelical church, a day care center, a busy road, and an apartment complex as a backdrop.

The bull's antlers are small and just beginning to come into velvet. Though he's young, his maleness, like that of a prize stallion, is visible and impressive. The animal lifts his head, staring down his funnel-like nose at us with seeming disdain, and studies the cluster of humans standing a few dozen yards away. Without a sound, the bull trots towards a thicket located at the south edge of the soccer complex.

"Jack," I shout to my youngest son as the moose glides majestically past the swing set, "see the moose?"

My son's small head, his hair newly clipped, his ears big and perky, emerges from the crow's nest at the top of the playground.

"Let's go see the moose," I hear Jack call to the little boy he's playing with.

Before I can intervene Jack is down the slide. My son plants his feet on the pea rock surrounding the playground and races across the U-6 soccer field towards the lumbering animal.

Mrs. Romano, the mom of one of the Hermantown players, retrieves a camera from her car. I inadvertently yell directly into her ear as she walks by. She doesn't say a word. Her attention is elsewhere.

"Jack," I shout, "get back on the swing set."

My son hears my voice. His head rotates in my direction. He stops in his tracks and considers the prancing exit of the big animal.

"Get back up on that swing set," I implore.

My son darts up the slide. His buddy follows suit. The moose shuffles its feet. Mrs. Romano snaps a few pictures before the animal decides he's had enough of humans and disappears into the brush behind the Community Church.

The crowd murmurs in amazement. The game resumes. It's obvious that the appearance of the moose, which the folks from Blaine probably believe is an every day occurrence in Hermantown, is too much for the boys from the Twin Cities. The Hermantown Havoc wins the game, going away without having to call upon their secret weapon to take a penalty kick.

Getting Away

Dylan, my eighteen year old son, and I dip our canoe paddles in the inky water of Brule Lake. It is after eight o'clock in the evening. There is a hint of dusk remaining beyond the rolling hills surrounding the western end of the lake. The sky is intermediate. Not high and distant. Not close and confining. There is no moon. The stars are masked.

We paddle in relative silence. Our eyes strain to identify the contours of the shoreline, islands, and reefs that disrupt the smooth plane of the water. Behind us my twenty-three year old son Matt and his friend Chris Oppel labor to keep up. Though both canoes are heavy with gear and the older boys are appreciably stronger than I am, Dylan and I make better time. I think our vessel's supremacy has something to do with my thirty-five years of manning the stern position in a canoe.

We drift next to a large island. The air is calm and without wind or rain. I study a Mackenzie map by headlamp. The lake is flat. No waves slap the gunwales of the canoe as I try to determine our location.

"You're welcome to pitch your tent with us," a woman calls out from the island.

By the texture of the voice, I'm guessing the speaker is in her early twenties. I hear other similar voices talking in low tones around her.

"We can't get our fire started," she adds.

It rained the prior evening. In reality, it was a deluge, the first significant storm since July. It's September, well beyond summer in Northeastern Minnesota. But until yesterday's rain it had been hot, muggy, and Kansas-like in the Northwoods for the majority of the past three months. Tonight is more typical of early September weather: cool, with an abundance of gray clouds.

"Maybe we should take them up on their offer," Dylan suggests.

I can't see my son's face but I suspect he's grinning from ear to ear. Matt hears the offer and joins in.

"Sounds like a good place to camp," Matt observes.

I mull over the woman's offer. Finding a group of desperate women in need of assistance was one of my fondest fantasies when I started coming to the Boundary Waters Canoe Area Wilderness with my high school buddies thirty years ago. However, such fantasies hold certain unacceptable risks for a forty-eight year old married father of four. My response is swift yet polite.

"Thanks for the offer, Ma'am. I think we'll keep looking."

"We tried all the campsites on the other islands and across the bay," she responds in a pleading tone. "They're all taken."

I smile. I sense the younger men in my group are not happy with their guide.

"All the same, I think we'll keep moving."

I study the map. The boys remain silent. I think they're mulling over whether mutiny is still a capital crime.

"There's an island in the middle of the lake that has a campsite on it," I advise.

Dylan resumes paddling. I adjust myself on the plastic seat and join in. The other canoe catches up and glides alongside us.

"I think that's the island," I say, pointing to a small clump of balsam, spruce, and undergrowth surrounded by exposed boulders.

"I dunno, dad," Dylan replies. "It looks too small."

"The map says there's a campsite here," I repeat.

We circle the island looking for the telltale clearing of a Forest Service-improved campsite.

"I don't think this is it," Matt says.

I dock the canoe at the only accessible point on the island. I hand Dylan a flashlight. He exits the canoe and disappears into the brush. Within minutes he's stumbling over deadfall trying to make it back to my location.

"There's no campsite here," he advises, struggling over rotting balsam logs.

We push off from shore and head towards Cone Bay. There's a distant glimmer visible across the water.

"That's a campsite," Dylan says, pointing to the flickering campfire.

"Looks like it's taken," I add. "There should be four more along the far shoreline. Hopefully one of them will be open."

Traveling at night across a lake as imposing as Brule in an open canoe is truly a spiritual experience, though I'm not so sure the boys share my sentimentality. We spend three hours exploring every inlet and nook of the northern shoreline of Brule Lake. It becomes clear that I'm wholly inept at coordinating the muted features of the landscape with the map on my lap.

"What about that bay?" I ask Matt as he and Chris negotiate a narrow passageway in the shoreline.

"Nothing there."

"Did you go to the end of it?"

"Nope," Matt says curtly.

Everyone's patience is wearing thin. It's after eleven. We need to set up camp, make dinner, and turn in. Tomorrow we're going to portage into a brook trout lake that Matt fished in the past with great success. Oodles of fat speckled trout are known to reside in the lake. I long to feel one of those storied fish on the end of my spinning rod.

"Dyl," I say, "let's take a peek. From the location of the campsite on the island," I continue, looking out across Cone Bay at the flickering campfire we left behind, "there should be a campsite on the left side of this bay."

Matt and Oppel remain out on the main body of water, convinced that our errand is another waste of time. Dylan and I paddle quietly through the night air. Fog settles over the placid surface of the bay. The only sound to be heard is the noise of water trickling off the blades of our paddles.

"What's over there?" Dylan asks, pointing at the marshy shoreline.

"Let's check it out," I urge.

The moon makes a brief appearance and illuminates the shoreline in yellow light. Thick clouds act as a reflective backdrop as we enter shallow water clogged with weeds.

Dylan leaps out of the canoe and threads his way through the undergrowth.

"It's a campsite, all right," he hollers.

"Matt," I yell out.

"Ya?"

"We found it."

The older boys land their Coleman canoe next to our Old Town Discovery as I'm unloading gear.

"You said there wasn't a campsite in here," I scold Matt.

"I said we didn't go to the end of the bay," he replies defensively.

"Same thing," I retort.

"Hey Dad," Matt interposes.

"Ya?" I say, swinging an overloaded Duluth Pack onto my shoulder.

"Tomorrow, let me carry the map."

Dawn comes early when you're sleeping on rock. Especially if you're middle-aged and bear the after effects of a spinal fusion. No matter how well designed a sleeping pad and sleeping bag you use, the fact is that the Canadian Shield, the rock which underlies all of the BWCA, is still rock. No amount of cushioning makes it any less so.

I awaken at dawn. The day is slightly overcast but without threat of rain. I get dressed, open the cooking kit, and lumber to the water's edge where I fill a coffee pot and two larger containers with water from the lake. I stretch the knots, tightening the muscles of my lower back, and scan the marsh around the small bay in front of me for signs of wildlife. Nothing stirs. I carry the water back to the campsite and light a single-burner propane stove. Escaping gas hisses. The blue flame pops after ignition. I place the coffee pot over heat.

Snoring emanates from the nylon dome tent where the three boys remain asleep. I drop water purification tablets into a pot full of water, shake the pot, and allow the water to settle before adding another tablet to disguise the chemical taste. This water is for fruit drink. It won't be boiled and though the water in most BWCA lakes is potable, I'm not willing to take chances. I allow the tablets to work before spooning heaps of instant drink into the pot.

The coffee is ready. I pour myself a cup, put another large pot of water on the burner, and stroll down to the water's edge. I find a weathered stump that fits my rear end and sit contentedly to watch the sun climb. After a few minutes of silent reflection I hear stirrings from the tent and I return to the campsite to prepare breakfast.

After a meal of instant oatmeal, breakfast bars (did you know you can get Cocoa Puffs and milk in a bar?), juice, and coffee, we load the canoes with fishing gear and begin the long paddle to the western terminus of Brule Lake, where high bluffs jut above the conifers and broadleaf trees of the forest. Here and there hints of fall color have painted the sugar maples. The real show is several weeks away but there is no question that autumn is just around the bend.

"It's across from those two points," I say, looking at the map once again.

I point to a narrow opening in the landscape as Dylan and I drift in the Old Town.

"You sure?" Matt asks.

"I'm sure," I assert.

Matt and Oppel paddle up.

"Through that gap," I say, pointing to a narrow passageway.

"That's how I remember it," Matt agrees.

The canoes round the point and head north through another channel.

"That's where we portage," Matt says, pointing to a huge cliff. The base of the ledge is littered with boulders loosened by ice and time. "But I don't see the path."

We inch closer to land. Tucked neatly to one side, just below a dip in the adjacent hillside, the portage trail appears. Our canoes drift into shore. Dylan and Oppel toss gear on their backs and begin the climb to the trout lake. Matt flips the Coleman canoe over, places a life jacket across his shoulders as a portage pad, lifts the canoe into place, and begins to trudge up the rocky path.

175

Despite back surgery I can still portage an average-sized canoe without any ill effect. Once Matt has a sufficient head start, I grab the gunwales of the Discovery, turn it over, and place the canoe on my shoulders in one motion. I begin a slow walk uphill. The portage trail winds up, up, and up through the trees. I concentrate on placing one hiking boot in front of the other as I climb.

"Doesn't this thing ever go down?" I hear Matt ask rhetorically after a few hundred yards of ascending the rocky trail.

"It has to," I answer, though I know he isn't talking to me.

"I don't think so," he replies. "Seems to me, the trout lake sits higher than Brule."

"Can't be. You must be remembering another lake."

Halfway up the slope, I find Matt and Oppel resting on a large balsam that was toppled by wind. The Coleman's prow rests on the tree completely blocking the path. Matt looks exhausted.

"Coming through," I say, passing the younger, stronger men on the trail.

It's not about strength, I think, *it's about balance. And stubbornness.*

"Show off," Matt mutters.

The trail is rough. It's clear that the United States Forest Service and the Minnesota Department of Natural Resources are not expending funds to maintain this portage. Boulders and rocks make for precarious footing. Downed balsams and spruce block the path at frequent intervals.

Still, I think, *if we get fish, it'll be worth it.*

Through a break in the foliage I catch glints of black water. As I crest the hill, the weight of the canoe begins to inflame my shoulders. Dylan meets me on the trail.

"Matt's right. It only goes up."

I refrain from answering.

We eat peanut butter and strawberry jam on pita bread for lunch on the rocky shore of the trout lake. We pass around a bag of beef jerky and drink orange Kool-Aid purified by iodine to quench our thirst. The clouds are high and unrelentingly pewter. The lake spreads out down a narrow valley between high bluffs. The shoreline is riddled with stones and boulders deposited by long departed glaciers.

"Someone caught some trout," Oppel notes, pointing to the skins of several nice brookies submerged in the lake in front of us. "At least the jerks could have put the evidence in the woods," I whisper, perturbed at the piggishness of some visitors to the BWCA.

Not that I am a saint. Years back, when I first came to the Wilderness, I too cleaned fish in the lakes and streams that I canoed. But no longer. The impact of leaving offal or garbage near campsites is clearly adverse to other folks enjoying the wilderness. Our wrappers and twist ties will be packed out with us. The innards of any fish we catch will be deposited away from the water, in the depths of the forest, where varmints can clean them up. Dishes are done in the same pots used for cooking and the gray water is spread on the ground so that our impact upon the land is minimized.

"Matt, I thought you said there were fish I this lake," I say as I toss a worm and jig into the deep water of the small lake.

As we fish, I form a theory about the remains we saw lying on the bottom of the lake. A front moving through piqued the interest of the lake's brook trout, rallying them from the doldrums of summer. Now the front is gone and the only evidence of fish is one small speckled trout that darts after my Mepp's Spinner but does not strike.

"There were lots of 'em. Big ones." Matt replies. "Maybe this is the wrong place."

"Wrong place?" I ask. "I don't think so. The portage was right where you said it should be."

"Still, I remember a big cliff. I don't see any cliffs."

We work our way to the western end of the lake. A bald eagle spreads its wings and leaves a dead white pine, its black and white coloring contrasting with the dull slate sky.

"Here's your cliff," I call out, landing the Discovery against the foot of a bluff, the majority of which is concealed behind a wall of cedars.

"Doesn't look like the place I remember," Matt stubbornly insists.

We catch no fish. We portage back to Brule Lake. At least we didn't leave any garbage behind as evidence.

A new day comes to Brule Lake on the heels of a brilliantly vacant sky. The sun rises over trees to the east and quickly warms the day beyond normal September temperatures. It's the last day of our three-day trek. My eldest sons, Matt and Dylan, and Matt's pal Chris Oppel remain fast asleep in our tent. I'm an early riser-I usually work on my writing at 6:ooam in the morning. Of course, I'm not writing anything in the woods. I'm working on making coffee over the hissing burner of a propane camp stove.

We came to Brule Lake in search of fish. The evening before, on our return from the "secret" trout lake we managed to run into oodles of small-mouthed bass along the craggy shoreline of the big lake.

"Look at that," Dylan had yelled out from the front seat of my Old Town Discovery canoe as a bass struck Dylan's spinner near the placid surface of Brule Lake.

Soon, both canoes were fighting churning, wheeling, darting bass of all shapes and sizes. I held a particularly large specimen landed by Dylan in my hands.

"This one will be great in the frying pan," I announced. "Nice fish, Dyl."

As I reached for my stringer, a thought occurred to me.

I wonder what the limit is?

I opened my tackle box, put the fish on the stringer, and tossed it over the gunwale of the canoe. I dug inside the box and found my DNR Fishing Regulations and thumbed through the pamphlet until I found what I was looking for.

"Oh oh," I muttered, dropping the booklet back into my tackle box.

I reached over the side and raised the stringer out of the water.

"What are you doing?" Matt yelled from out from the other canoe as I slid the big fish off the stringer into Brule Lake.

I ignored my son's question, hoping that common sense would take over.

"Why are you letting Dyl's fish go?" Matt continued.

Dylan understood what I was doing and placed an index finger to his lips. I could see the light bulb go off inside Matt's head as if he was a character in a Saturday morning cartoon.

"Oh," Matt finally said. "I get it."

"Season closed two days ago," I said. "We can catch 'em but we can't keep 'em."

There is no wind this morning. The air warms quickly. In summer, our campsite on this dead end bay would be swarming with mosquitoes and flies of every configuration. But because it's September, there are no bugs. Not a one. My trek down to the lake to fill up assorted pots with water for breakfast is pleasantly devoid of insects.

The boys get up. Our breakfast of instant oatmeal (a new variety that comes complete with dehydrated fruit), breakfast bars, hot coffee, cocoa, and Kool-Aid goes down quickly. By mid-morning our gear is stowed in the canoes. I invert my water-repellent oilskin bush hat to haul water to douse the campfire. Hot embers sputter and spew steam as I extinguish the last remnants of flame. A quick reconnoiter of the campsite reveals that we have followed the guidelines of the BWCA. We're leaving the campsite cleaner than we found it.

We fish the calm waters of the lake and land bass after bass, releasing them as soon as they reach the canoes. Some of the fish are smaller than the lures they chase after. Some would be fine specimens for the frying pan. All of them seek the warm waters of Brule Lake upon release.

"Catchin' anything other than bass?" I ask two guys in a square stern AlumaCraft canoe anchored off a rocky point typical of the landscape to be found throughout border country.

"Nope. Just bass."

"Lookin' for a campsite?" I ask, recalling the difficulties we faced finding a place to set up our tent two nights earlier.

"Just in for the day," the man's companion advises.

"Good luck," I say before paddling away.

We enter a large bay that, according to the map on my lap, should be near where we entered Brule Lake two days earlier.

"I think the landing is straight ahead," I tell Dylan as we strain to out-paddle Matt and Oppel.

An informal race begins. Unfortunately, we're headed in the wrong direction.

"I think we're supposed to follow that guy in the kayak," Matt says, pointing out yet again that I'm illiterate when it comes to reading a map.

The two older boys shoot ahead. Dylan and I come about. Matt is in the stern of the red canoe. He sets a straight line for an opening in the shoreline, an opening, which, upon closer inspection, leads to the boat landing.

"Dig in," I admonish Dylan. "We'll take them on the inside."

Using years of canoe experience to out-fox my eldest son, I cut inside the contending canoe. Dylan pulls mightily. My left shoulder, a joint that has given me trouble since high school, aches as I dig my custom-made paddle into the lake.

"Gotcha," I exclaim as we pass Matt and his buddy and cut them off from shore.

The prow of the Discovery slides into soft sand. Our brief stay in wilderness is over. I'm tired and sore as I help load the canoes and our gear into my Honda Passport and its attached utility trailer.

As I settle in behind the steering wheel of the SUV, it occurs to me that I might want to pick up some walleye fillets on the way home.

Jack's Swing Set

"Jack really needs a play gym," my wife announced as she surveyed the vast emptiness of our backyard, a closely mown pasture that slopes gently to the edge of the Cloquet River.

"I know," I responded, fully aware that, when we sold our old farmhouse, the first play gym I'd constructed for our three eldest sons remained behind as part of the sale.

"Well, when are you planning on getting to it?"

I knew better than to utter a response.

"I was thinking maybe next Saturday you could put it up," Rene added, not waiting for my reply.

"I guess I'll be working on it next Saturday, then won't I?" I replied.

We had already selected the particular unit at Menard's that seemed to fit the bill. The package included a tower, two swings, a rock climbing wall, and assorted other stations in one fairly compact structure. The cost for the hardware and all of the lumber was around $500.00.

René borrowed her dad's truck to pick up the wood and the accessories. When she pulled onto our back lawn in the little red Chevrolet S-10 two-wheel-drive pickup, the back end of the truck scraped grass. Green treated lumber was piled in the box of the vehicle to the limits of the topper.

"Is all that for this project?" I asked incredulously.

"Yep," my spouse responded, alighting from the truck with Christian.

"Lot's to cut, eh Dad?" my teenager chided through a smile.

I scanned the stack of lumber.

Lot's indeed, I thought.

"The box says it only takes five to seven hours to put together," Rene advised as she and Chris removed packages from the back of the truck.

I stared hard at the printed information on the cardboard carton. She was right, at least as far as the bold print was concerned.

"You didn't read the fine print," I observed.

"How's that?" Rene asked.

"The fine print underneath the '5-7 hours' says that's contractor time."

"Oh."

My wife offered no further commentary as she headed towards the house.

Standing in summer light, the wind still, the heat meager, I read the instructions.

"Here's what I'm gonna do," I said to Chris, who was kneeling next to me, as Jack danced around the pile, excited as all get out that his long-promised swing set was about to be constructed.

"What's that?" the teenager replied.

"Donate a buck to the church for every time I swear building this thing."

Chris smiled.

"You don't have that much money," Chris observed as he walked away.

The time estimate on the box was right, that is, if you're only counting the amount of time it takes to saw the lumber. The wood wasn't precut. I had to measure and trim every piece to be used. From that standpoint, the instructions were accurate. After six hours, I'd created a pile of pieces ready to be bolted together. I didn't utter one swear word during the process. The church was in jeopardy of being impoverished.

Sunday after worship, I began to assemble the main structure, the posts, the sandbox and the roof for the center tower, the place where Jack would pretend he was King Richard the III defending his domain against insurgents. By nightfall, I was only half-way through the assembly process and the church was three dollars ahead of the game. Total time spent to that point: sixteen hours.

Monday and Tuesday evenings, instead of watching the magical swirl of the Cloquet River or trying my hand at walleye fishing on nearby Island Lake, I worked on the play gym. Two more dollars were donated to Trinity Episcopal Church when I found the first and only major glitch in the quality of my construction. A plastic piece meant to fit between two posts as a *faux* rock ladder couldn't be anchored. A few curse words, some heady thinking and the gap was bridged by another post, allowing the ladder to be secured.

As stars began to twinkle Tuesday evening, I poured bags of mason's sand into the base of the tower completing the job. The swings were attached. The climbing ropes, slide, and other accessories were secured in place. Remarkably, the thing appeared level and plumb from every angle.

"That looks great," René admitted, expressing genuine awe at my new found construction prowess.

I kept my thoughts to myself.

"That really wasn't so bad now was it?"

I gnawed on the inside of my mouth.

"Twenty-three," I mumbled.

"What?"

"Twenty-three," I repeated, picking up tools scattered across dry grass.

"What are you talking about?"

"The box said 'five to seven hours'. It took me twenty-three hours to put up this...." I paused, not wishing to owe the church any more money, "blessed thing," I concluded.

Behind me, my youngest son squealed with joy as he clambered up the slide.

"How can you put a price on that?" my very wise significant other asked, forcing me to turn to watch Jack's antics.

My wife's rhetorical question drew no argument from me.

Wild Minnesota

It seems that my life compels me to rush. I never have the time, or perhaps, I'm so blinded by my obsessive nature, that I never take the time to relax. It's kind of pointless to trout fish if your mind isn't on the river. Despite this flaw in my personality, I still like to get away up the North Shore of Lake Superior in search of brook trout.

There are four trout species, not counting hybrids, that one can catch in Minnesota. German brown trout, rainbow trout (called steelheads when they occupy Lake Superior and return to the coastal rivers to spawn), lake trout, and brook or speckled trout are the four varieties. Of the four, only brook trout and lake trout are native to Minnesota. Before 1900, brook trout were limited by geography to Lake Superior itself and to those stretches of rivers, streams, and creeks between the lake and the first natural barrier (falls or rapids) located inland from Lake Superior's shoreline. That there are now native populations of propagating brookies above the first barrier in nearly every trickle of black water flowing from the interior of Northeastern Minnesota is due to man's intervention: the artificial planting of that native species above the first waterfall or rapids during the late 19th and early 20th centuries.

My Honda Passport, a small SUV that I bought used and curse often, bounces along the blacktop highway threading the backwoods towards the North Shore from my home north of Duluth. It's an early Friday morning in July. The sun is beginning to rise in the east above the green leaves of aspen and birch, and the feathered crowns of second-growth pines and spruce. There's not a cloud in the sky. Given my schedule as a District Court Judge, a vacation day during the week is a rare and pleasurable treat. But the day, one that is clear of rain and clouds, selected months in advance, does not foreshadow success on the water.

I'm determined to find the upper reaches of the Beaver River, a place noted for solid, if not spectacular, brook trout fishing. As you know from reading other tales of angling misadventure from my pen, I'm almost exclusively a worm dunker. On rare occasions when overwrought by shame I will resort to using artificial flies to tempt fish. Not today. Today, a day of leisure crammed between days of economic production, I will use worms. I want to catch fish. I nearly always do so when I use worms.

A tiny ribbon of asphalt hued water courses beneath the logging road. To the left side of the road, the landscape opens into a marshy plain. The place has all the look and feel of a beaver pond. Beaver ponds can, during their early stages of existence, before the water warms and silts up, hold fat trout.

I park the car by the side of the primitive trail and open the vehicle's rear hatch. The air is warm. The sky is open and silver blue. The sun glows. Fishing will be problematic. I pull on my neoprene waders, rig my fly rod (a cheap eight footer) with a hook, some split shot sinkers, and a small portion of night crawler. I snug my battered Australian bush hat down on my head, the brim sloped in multiple directions from the abuse it's seen over the years, and head down the ditch bank towards the creek.

The stream bed is solid. There is ample gravel to support my weight as I begin wading downstream towards the open area to the east. I toss and retrieve the worm along the banks of the brook. Here and there, small chubs break free of the water and clamp down hard on the free food, only to break off once I haul them from the water into open air. I catch no trout. I do not feel the tell-tale strike of a game fish. Only the nibble, nibble, nibble of pesky minnows.

The country opens up. At the far end of the clearing, perhaps a hundred yards from my position, a beaver dam blocks the downward flow of the modest creek. A shimmering pool of dark water has collected behind the artificial obstacle. The going becomes difficult. Hummocks of marsh grass, undulating piles of soggy earth interspaced with holes of brackish backwater, lace the perimeter of the pond, making forward progress a chore. I begin to sweat. Flies buzz my head, but thanks to my thick oilskin hat, they cannot bite.

After fifteen minutes of plunging, slipping, teetering, and nearly submerging, I claim a small point of land jutting out into the pond. I gingerly probe the murky water with a stick. The pond bottom is silty but solid. I step into the water. The stream bed holds my weight. I begin casting towards trouty places. I catch no fish but for the first time since leaving home, I feel the weight of my job, of marriage, of fatherhood, of trying to be a writer in my spare time, lighten. It's as if someone has filled my soul with just a whiff of helium.

Here and there songbirds flit and trill. I am not much of an ornithologist. I can't identify more than a few of the birds that inhabit the woods and swamps of this part of the world. I know the call of the robin, the voice of the red-winged blackbird, the chatter of the kingfisher. Beyond that, I'm pretty much clueless. An osprey glides into view, its wings outstretched, its voice distinctive and clear. The sun climbs. Fragments of cloud drift across the aqua and blue vault. These inconsequential pieces of fluff are high and fragile. I wish that were not so. I wish they were rain clouds gathering to spill. That would help the fishing. But there is no rain in the forecast and certainly none in the sky.

Beyond the occasional bird call the woods are silent. There is no wind. I continue to work the near shoreline of the pond, pulling my waders free of the oozy bottom, loosening clouds of brown silt with each step.

A crash. A loud noise off to the east towards the far side of the beaver dam. My heart races. I hold my breath. I know this much from my nearly fifty years of life and an almost equal time in the bush: There are only two animals in northeastern Minnesota capable of making that much noise in the forest.

She doesn't see me at first. Her spindly legs clamber over the beaver dam. She steps into the deepest part of the pond with a grace that defies her size. Though some would consider her face, her large snout and loose neck to be less than attractive, a cow moose is an impressive and beautiful creature when she's standing twenty feet away chest deep in water. Her eyes focus on me. It's clear she knows I'm here.

186

She doesn't seem concerned by the small human mired in the muck of the pond. In reality, if she chose to charge me, out of curiosity or fear, I'd be a sitting duck. She'd be able to cover the distance between us in two strides. With my boots buried in the pond bottom she'd bowl me over like one of those sand filled inflatable punching bags we played with when we were kids. I watch her carefully to insure my assessment is correct. She lowers her head, flies circling the thick fir of her back and rear, and moves steadily away from me in search of food.

For fifteen minutes I watch the cow eat. She never looks back, never acknowledges my presence after that first furtive glance. When she finally clambers off into the thick brush on the far shore, there is no mistaking the sound of a moose in the woods.

Later that same day, as I drive north on Highway 2 towards Isabella, a bull moose canters out in front of the Honda nearly striking a southbound Toyota in what seems like an urgent and ill-advised rush to cross the highway. Despite the fact that the bull is only fifty yards in front of the oncoming car as it crosses the blacktop, the car never slows.

How can you not see a moose on a highway? I wonder as the animal clears the ditch and disappears into the thicket.

I turn off Highway 2 and follow a primitive logging trail in search of better water. As I round the bend in the gravel road, a large animal lopes onto the path, stops, and rears itself on its hind legs. A black bear stands fat and ominous in the middle of the road watching the Honda intently as I brake and place the vehicle in park. Satisfied that the car poses no threat, the boar lowers itself onto all fours and vanishes into the undergrowth in a fashion reminiscent of dead ball players disappearing into a mythical Iowa cornfield.

When I've fished enough to weary my bones and satisfy my lust, I head home. I catch one brook trout, a six inch gleaming gem of color right in front of the beaver dam that I landed just before the cow moose joined me in the pond. I let the fish go realizing that God did not intend for me to catch trout on this day, that there were other matters on His or Her agenda for me to consider.

A Rainy Day

"**W**here's Copper?" I ask my eldest son Matt as we sit at the kitchen table. "I haven't seen him in a while."

The question references our three year old yellow Labrador retriever. A big, friendly dog, Copper usually stays close to home unless drawn into an excursion by our other "outside" dog, a black Labrador mix named Daisy. The standing joke around the house is: that if both big dogs are left unrestrained, Daisy takes off with the yellow dog trotting cheerfully behind her, vanishing for a day or so. The speculation is that Daisy's motivation for these treks is not altruistic: she's trying to get Copper lost so she has the place all to herself.

"I haven't seen him since Sunday," Matt replies. "He followed Kelly and me up the river when we went for a canoe ride."

"Where did you last see him?"

"He was in Kaas's yard."

Barb and Jim Kaas live next door to us, in the old Sears farmhouse we sold to them. It's plausible, given the collection of horses and dogs assembled at the Kaas place, that Copper is simply visiting our neighbors.

My third son Chris wanders upstairs from his bedroom clad only in boxer shorts.

"Chris, have you seen Copper?"

"Not since Sunday."

"Matt says the dog followed him up the river when he and Kelly went canoeing. Daisy's home so he's not with her."

"I haven't seen him," Chris affirms, reaching into the cupboard for a box of cereal.

I walk to the front room window and watch drizzle fall softly on the lush green of our lawn. June has been a rainy month, the kind of June I recall from my youth. The past few years, June has brought little rain and stifling heat, meaning that Island Lake and the other area lakes fed by the Cloquet and Beaver Rivers have been low, causing the year-round residents on the lakes to complain to Minnesota Power, the

188

corporate entity controlling the water level, to cease releasing water into the rivers. This year, the summer skies have opened up to quiet the complainers.

"You'll need to post pictures and information about Copper at the Minno-ette," I say to Chris, referring to our local gas station and convenience store. I hold a hot cup of coffee in my hand as I stand in the front entry and watch the rain through a screen door. "He probably wandered all the way up to Island Lake. Some family is keeping him until they figure out where he came from."

Chris grumbles as he pours milk over his Frosted Mini-Wheats. Knowing his connection to the lost dog, I'm certain he'll post the notices.

I leave for work. By the time I come home there are posters up in all the local bars and convenience stores. No one calls about the dog.

The rain continues through Wednesday. Given that we've heard nothing about the dog, I begin to suspect the worst. A few days back, Chris rode our battered old Yamaha four wheeler up the trail along the south bank of the River, near where Matt last saw the dog, but found no evidence of the missing Labrador. When I come home from work on Wednesday, I decide to search for the dog myself. I'm not optimistic. The realization that Copper likely never made it further than the Taft Road, the road that passes in front of the Kaas place, hangs over me like a pall. I'm saddened by the thought. Copper has been a good companion to my boys, especially Chris. I remember back to the day Chris and I first saw Copper's yellow puppy face staring at us from the top of the riverbank as we paddled home from a trip down the Cloquet River. That pup grew into an affectionate, obedient, gentle giant. Lately, with the addition of Jimi, my wife's miniature dachshund, to our family, Copper has found a new playmate. Though he outweighs Jimi by seventy-five pounds, Copper allows the pesky wiener dog to bite his ears, nip at his loose skin, and generally be a pest. When Copper's had enough, the big dog simply slaps a paw on Jimi's head and pins him, gently holding the puppy still until the little dog gets the message. Copper, when all things that matter in a dog are measured, has become one of the best Labs we've ever owned.

I dress in old jeans and a sweatshirt before pulling rain pants and a matching green poncho over my clothes. The rain attacks the roof of the front porch of our house as I sit on an old rocking chair and tighten the laces of my hiking boots. I decide against using the four-wheeler, figuring I can cover more ground on foot than I can if I'm restricted to trails.

My heart is heavy as I start on my quest to find the missing dog. The rain intensifies. A steady pulse of clean, warm water strikes my rain suit as I leave the porch. I find no dog tracks in the mud of the access road leading to our house. I see no evidence of Copper.

I pause at the intersection of our road, the Knutsen Road, and the Taft Road, the two-lane county road that is the major traffic artery through our township. Big dollops of rain splash against warm tar as I cross Taft. I follow the same trail that Chris had driven a few days earlier. I climb a small knoll. My eyes scan the underbrush, the vegetation sparse and easily scrutinized due to the presence of large white and red pines. The trees' canopy precludes the incursion of alder. I walk a few steps along the ridge before I find our missing dog.

At first, I do not recognize him. Two or three days of summer heat have made Copper's muscular torso bloat to the size of a St. Bernard. His collar isn't visible. The dog's neck is so swollen that his collar has disappeared beneath inflated skin. I stop. I want to cry but, for some inexplicable reason, I can't. It's a scene, living in the country, that I have confronted all too often. Dead dogs. Dead cats. Dead horses. I have buried a Noah's ark of animals in the dirt of our land. Copper is just the latest in a long list of four-legged companions to have met his end living along the banks of the Cloquet River.

I kneel next to Copper and stroke his fur. It's clear from the wounds on his flank that he was struck by a car when he tried to cross the road. Copper, his life leaving him quickly, managed to crawl to a place of sanctuary, a sheltered nest beneath a huge white pine, protected from the rain, nearly invisible from the trail. I sigh, but still, I do not cry.

When I walk up our driveway to get the four-wheeler and its trailer, Chris is standing beneath the roof of the front porch. From the slowness of my gait, he knows.

"You found him?"

"Yes."

"Where?"

"Next to the trail going up the River. Underneath the big pines."

"I drove by there."

"I know. He was a ways off the trail. Must have crawled there. You stay here. You don't want to see him like this."

Chris doesn't say a word as I hitch the trailer to the Yamaha and pull the starter rope on the four-wheeler. The Yamaha coughs, then dies. I pull the rope again, flutter the throttle. The engine catches, then idles.

The dog is heavy and wet as I gather him in my arms and place him in the bed of the trailer. I drive slowly. I am filled with reverence, not urgency, as I head back to the house.

Parking the trailer on the driveway, I walk past Christian and enter the foyer of our home. My son braves the weather to see his dog. I can only surmise that tears mix with warm rain as Chris silently contemplates his dead friend.

"He's gone," I tell my wife René as she stands behind the kitchen island preparing dinner.

"Copper?"

"Yes. He must have tried to follow Matt up the River. He never made it past the road."

"He was a good dog."

I leave it to my wife to relay the news to our youngest boy, Jack. At seven, the dog's passing will likely hit him hard. Sexist as it might sound, a mother's sensitivity is warranted in breaking such news to someone so young.

I walk back to the trailer. Chris looks away from his pal. His slender torso shudders. He follows the four-wheeler to the place I've chosen for Copper's grave. I turn off the Yamaha, grab a No. 2 shovel, and begin to dig. My son stands next to me for a moment before turning to escape the sadness.

191

It's only after I've patted the last of the muddy soil over Copper with the shovel that I allow tears to finally come.

Other Works by the Author

The Legacy (ISBN 0972005021; Cloquet River Press)
Set against the backdrop of WWII Yugoslavia and present-day Minnesota, this debut novel combines elements of military history, romance, thriller, and mystery. Rated 3 and 1/2 daggers out of 4 by *The Mystery Review Quarterly*.

River Stories (ISBN 0972005013; Cloquet River Press)
A collection of essays describing life in Northern Minnesota with a strong emphasis on the out-of-doors, the rearing of children, and the environment. A mixture of humor and thought-provoking prose gleaned from the author's columns in *The Hermantown Star*.

Ordinary Lives (ISBN 0972005005; Cloquet River Press)
Creative fiction from one of Northern Minnesota's newest writers, these stories touch upon all elements of the human condition and leave the reader asking for more.

Pigs, a Trial Lawyer's Story (ISBN 097200503x; Cloquet River Press)
A story of a young trial attorney, a giant corporation, marital infidelity, moral conflict, and choices made, *Pigs* takes place against the backdrop of Western Minnesota's beautiful Smokey Hills. This tale is being compared by reviewers to Grisham's best.

Suomalaiset: People of the Marsh (ISBN 0972005064; Cloquet River Press)
A dockworker is found hanging from a rope in a city park. How is his death tied to the turbulence of the times? A masterful novel of compelling history and emotion, *Suomalaiset* has been hailed by reviewers as a "must read".

Order Direct from Cloquet River Press at:
www.cloquetriverpress.com
Order direct from our estore at the website!

The Author Fishing the Betsy River in Michigan

About the Author

Mark Munger is a District Court Judge serving four counties in Northeastern Minnesota. When not on the bench, Mark lives on the banks of the wild and scenic Cloquet River with his wife René and their four sons. Though Mark no longer writes his bi-weekly column, "Living Out" for the *Hermantown Star*, he continues to work on extended fiction and non-fiction projects. He is currently researching the background of noted Minnesota environmentalist (and uncle) Willard Munger for a biography and is also in the process of writing his fourth novel.

You can email Mark with your comments about this book or his other writing at: cloquetriverpress@yahoo.com.